Half Gone

Orange Books Publication

1st Floor, Rajhans Arcade, Mall Road, Kohka, Bhilai, Chhattisgarh 490020
Website: **www.orangebooks.in**

First Edition, 2025

ISBN: 978-93-6554-260-8

Price: Rs. 295.00

Printed in India

Half GONE

Medha Veliganti

Orange Books Publication
www.orangebooks.in

To Sara ma'am, my first and favourite English teacher

Index

Chapter – 1

Newspaper clipping from 2005

The Dispatch Daily

October 1, 2005

Highway Tragedy: Two Family Members Killed and One Missing After September 21 Incidents

A heart-wrenching incident on September 21 saw two members of an affluent Indian family die in a tragic highway collision. Around 9:03 PM on Route 16, thc family's vehicle was violently struck head-on by a cargo lorry. The driver had fled the scene.

The Singh family, comprising Anish Singh and his wife Alisha Singh, forty-two and forty years of age, respected doctors in their community, along with their two daughters, aged fifteen and ten, Sanya and Sara, were returning home following a happy outing when disaster struck. The night has been described as foggy, with reduced visibility and wet roads due to rain at the time of the catastrophe.

Emergency services reached the accident site about an hour after the accident occurred. The time was approximately 10:09 PM. The paramedics did an intense job in saving some members of the family severely injured. However, due to the late arrival of paramedics, both Anish and Alisha could not be saved and were pronounced dead right on the scene. Impact also left Sara, the younger daughter, fighting for life, but she survived. In the mayhem, Sanya was allegedly said to have run into the nearby forest, named Crimson Woods; it was suspected she ran off in a daze, and was actively bleeding. Despite extensive search efforts on the part of local authorities and community volunteers, to date, she has still not been found, leaving a haunting void in this family tragedy.

The local authorities have launched an investigation into the incident and are actively hunting the cargo lorry, which apparently fled the scene after this collision, and the search for the young fifteen – year - old Sanya Singh continues. According to reports from eyewitnesses, after the collision, it is believed that the lorry took a turn to head southeast of London in the direction of Hastings. The community is in mourning and is appealing to the people to remain vigilant and inform the authorities of any suspicious activity or possible sightings. Community support is considered an essential aspect of resolving the case soon and bringing justice to the Singh family. Anyone with information, contact 1603-1410 or the nearest police station immediately.

PART- 1

20 years later.

8:15 pm

Sara slammed her phone on the table as she leaned back in her chair; her head was spinning from all the patients she had operated on. Three kids and four adults a day, not quite fun. She sighed as she picked up her laptop and put it on her desk and then flipped it open. The flickering screen illuminated her tired, dark eyes. She scrolled through her patient log, trying to find her next operation. Her eyes landed on a patient file, and she clicked on it. She yawned. "Okay, focus", she mumbled to herself. She squinted her eyes as she read the details of her patient to refresh her memory "In and out in 90 minutes", she mumbled to herself as she walked out into the hallway. She looked at her watch. She walked to the operating theatre, and she smiled seeing the nurses. "Hello," she walked with them as they showed her the patient's vitals. Sara nodded. Everything looked good. The anesthesiologist walked out of the operating room and waved at Sara, "Patient is good to go, all set." Sara nodded as she scrubbed her hands, and a nurse put gloves on her. "Where is Doctor Ray? He was supposed to be here by now" Sara glanced around, looking for her colleague. A nurse put Sara's surgical mask on, "He's already in the operating room, doctor." Sara nodded and walked in. "Hello, doctor Ray", she said as she stood opposite him, the patient lying in front of them. "Hey, so this surgery is quick, it's just an appendectomy, should be over in an hour or so, everyone ready?" The nurses and Sara nodded. The operation began. As the surgery started, the operating room went quiet, except for the quiet humming of the machinery and rhythmic beeping of monitors, "Doctor Sara, do you want to make the initial incision, or shall I?" Sara looked up, she nodded and took the scalpel from the sterile tray, just as she maneuvered the scalpel to make the incision, the door swung open. Doctor Ray turned to the door, angry, he was going to say something about the sudden entry, when the nurse who came in spoke, "I'm so sorry, but Doctor Sara, there is an emergency, you must leave now." Sara looked confused, "What? Is it another patient?" The nurse sighed ", No, someone wants you to come down." Doctor Ray interrupted, "Is it more important than this surgery that she has to leave just before we started?"

The nurse looked away, "Doctor, the person who asked me to call you said someone died." Sara's eyes widened, "Died?" She repeated.

The nurse nodded. Sara looked down. She didn't have any family. The family she had they were dead. Almost two decades ago, in an accident, her mother and father died, and her sister, she never knew where she ran off to. She has been missing till date; at this point, she is likely dead. That's what the police told her after they gave up on the search for her in Crimson Woods. "Do you know who died?" Sara asked the nurse as she walked out of the operating room. The nurse nodded no. Sara sighed as she threw her gloves in the trash and walked down to the lobby, where the person had been waiting. "Where is the person who came for me?" She asked, looking at the nurse. The nurse walked around the hospital lobby, her eyes tensed up, "She was here just before I came to get you, Doctor." Sara exhaled as she held her forehead, "Please don't interrupt me like that in the middle of a surgery, I was about to begin." The nurse interrupted her, "Doctor, she was crying and asking for you, saying someone died, she looked homeless, she had dark brown hair and black eyes, she looked familiar, almost" Sara tilted her head "Homeless? She must be some crazy lady." The nurse sighed, "I'm sorry, she looked desperate." Sara nodded, and the nurse walked off.

Homeless? Sara didn't know anyone, she didn't really have friends either, being a doctor, she had to sacrifice it all, friends, fun, family-

Sara looked at her watch, 9:10. Her shift at the hospital would be over in 40 minutes; she couldn't go back to perform the surgery. Doctor Ray must have already started. She sighed and stepped into the elevator and clicked on the fifth floor, where her office was. The elevator music played in her ears as she zoned out, thinking about who the lady was. Sara closed her eyes, trying to remember if she knew someone who was homeless, with dark brown hair and black eyes. Ah, yes, she did. Her eyes brightened up. She had undergone surgery two months ago, she was shot by another homeless person, and the police brought her in. But why was she back? Maybe to thank Sara? Maybe.

The elevator music stopped as it reached the fifth floor. Sara stepped out, walked to her office, grabbed her bag and slid her laptop in, she walked out and locked the door. She checked her watch. 9:20. Twenty more minutes till her shift was over. She walked back to the elevator and pressed ‘B’, basement. The music filled her ears again, and she leaned against the walls and held her head. She had a migraine. “Stupid shift”, she mumbled as the elevator stopped as it reached the basement. The basement was empty, dark and hot. Sara made her way to her car, parked at the very end, her neck was clammy and sweaty as she wiped sweat off her forehead. Her steps echoed off the basement walls. She took her bag and looked for her car keys. As she reached her car, she fumbled with her keys, her hand slightly trembling. Weird, it wasn’t cold in the basement. She unlocked her car, threw her bag in the back, and walked to the front. Footsteps, she heard more footsteps. She turned back to see who it was. No one. Sara felt a cool breeze hit the back of her neck. She turned around again, staring at the empty basement. She turned back to her car, got in the driver's seat, and pulled out of her slot. She slammed on the gas and went out of the basement. The London air hit her as she drove out of the basement and rolled her windows down. She saw the hospital security standing at the exit. "Hey, Mr. Dawn!" She waved at him, "You're clocking out of your shift early today?" he asked, checking his watch, his eyebrows lowering. "Oh, yes, I'm feeling sick", she replied with a fake frown, trying to sound convincing; her throat tingled. "Well, take care, Miss", he said, a warm smile breaking through, "Make sure you rest up." Sara nodded and smiled as she drove away; she could feel the weight of his gaze lingering on her back. She wasn't sick. The streets blurred past her as she drove. She manoeuvred through the traffic. Pulling into the parking lot of her apartment complex, she took a moment to breathe the fresh air. Her apartment was big, a three-bedroom unit on the eighth floor with a view of the city skyline. The walls were painted a soft beige, and the living room was adorned with a few framed photos from happier times. As she stepped inside, the door creaked slightly, and the familiar scent of her home, a mix of lavender and the faint aroma of antiseptic from her scrubs, filled her nose. Sara dropped her bag on the kitchen counter and walked into the living room to take her shoes off, where a large framed photograph caught her eye. She smiled as she walked towards it. It was a daily ritual. It was a family portrait. Taken years back before the accident that shattered her world. In the picture, she stood between her parents, with her sister on her right side; they were all beaming with joy. Alisha looked beautiful next to her husband and two daughters. Sanya's head was tilted, and her dark black eyes shone. Anish, their dad, was looking slightly at his wife while smiling at her. Sara's mother's arms were wrapped around her, and her father stood next to his older daughter. Sara smiled as she touched the photo, her fingers brushing on the glass frame as she gazed at their faces, the memories flooding back: family dinners, long drives, game nights, laughter echoing through the house, the warmth of their love. But that warmth had been snuffed out. She became a doctor, just like her parents, that was the one thing they would have wanted for her.” I love you all so much", she whispered. The words hung in the air. Sara walked to the kitchen and poured herself a glass of water. She looked out the big windows as the city's night lights shone outside. She sat down after washing up and turned on the TV. She sank into her couch as the soft hum of the TV filled the room. She was just getting comfortable when her doorbell rang. Sara flinched, “Who is it now?” she muttered, getting up, annoyed. She set her remote down and walked to the door. She swung the door open. No one. She looked around the empty hallway. She stood there for a moment. She looked annoyed and shut her door and went back to her couch. She settled down when she heard a noise outside. Sara's ears perked up. Maybe it was the neighbours, or the wind, or a stupid prank from the neighbours’ kids. She heard it again, a soft scratching sound at her door. She walked to the door and swung it open again. No one. The hallway was still and quiet. She slammed her door and locked it. She turned the TV off and lay down on the couch, as she slowly fell asleep, the city lights gleaming through the night sky in the big windows.

Chapter – 2

6:07 am

The alarm rang in Sara's ears, and she stumbled off the couch she had fallen asleep in. She yawned as she stretched her arms. She squinted her eyes as she stared at her phone. 6:10. She was going to be late. Again. She fell asleep on the couch, which happened a lot. She was too tired to go back and sleep on the bed. She exhaled loudly as she went to her bathroom, half asleep.

She stepped out of the bathroom, her mouth still lingering the fresh smell of toothpaste, she changed into new scrubs and combed her black hair. She put it back into a slick ponytail and walked to the kitchen. She poured herself a mix of instant coffee when the doorbell rang. "I swear, if this is another stupid prank, and no one is there", she walked to the door and opened it slowly. No one. Again. She looked at her doorbell. "Maybe it's malfunctioning, I should get it checked out by the technician later", her eyes drifted down. A small brown cardboard box, with a red envelope on top, was lying on top of her mat. "Must be the neighbours" " she picked it up and turned it around to find the address. Nothing. It was just a box with an envelope on it. She sighed and took it in and placed it on her table. "I don't have time for this", she mumbled as she opened the letter

Watch out. You'll pay for it. My life was ruined, now I'll ruin yours.

Sara threw the envelope aside. It was a prank. It must be. What had she done?

She was just an overworked surgeon with no friends. Well, she did have a friend, Officer Rosalia, her police officer friend. They met a long time ago, when Sara performed surgery on Rosalia's son. He wouldn't have survived if it weren't for Sara. Rosalia promised she would be there for Sara all the time to protect her.

Sara shook her head. Rosalia wouldn't play a prank like this; she was a busy woman, just like her. She took the box and opened it up. "Oh my-"

There were 5 pictures of Sara. But Sara didn't take them. It was like a stalker took them. Sara winced. The first picture was of her at the start of her shift at 7:00 am in the break room, drinking coffee, the second was of her parking her car in the basement, the third was of her talking to a patient outside her office, the forth was of her coming down in the middle of surgery when the nurse told her someone wanted to meet her, and the last picture was one of her in the basement, leaving the hospital. Sara's eyes widened. She had heard footsteps in the basement. She wasn't imagining it; someone was actually there. Her palms got sweaty as she dropped the pictures on the kitchen counter. She stared at the letter she had thrown aside; it looked familiar. The handwriting, but she couldn't place it. "Oh my god, someone is following me," she whispered. A realisation hit her like a bullet. "Wait, if they sent the pictures here, that means they know where I live-" her eyes widened, she held her forehead and looked around her apartment. "I can't go to the hospital today", she mumbled, as she texted her head doctor that she was not coming. She got up and changed into a flannel shirt and jeans. "I need to report this to the police", She grabbed her keys and purse and walked out of her apartment. She looked around the empty hallways. Whoever was stalking her they were here. She ran to the elevator and pressed the button, looking around as she broke into a sweat. "Oh, come on", she pressed the elevator button again, her thumb clenching against it. "I'll take the stairs then" She ran down the stairs, to her apartment parking lot and jumped into her car Her heart was pounding as she pulled out of the parking lot. She drove to the station where her friend worked. She jumped out of the car, slamming the door. Her eyes were dark and bloodshot. She ran up to the police station and swung the doors open. Her heart raced as she entered, the fluorescent lights buzzing over her. She saw some officers huddled over paperwork, and some near the reception. Her eyes scanned through the officers as she tried to find Rosalia. "Where is she…" she said, walking to the reception. She leaned font on the table, "Hey, I'm looking for Officer Rosalia." The officer sitting at the desk looked up, her light blue eyes shot up to Sara, "Why?" she asked, scrunching her nose. "I need to meet her…to tell her about something"

The officer sighed, her grey hair shone in the lights above her, "What is that something?"

"Someone is stalking me."

"Okay, you should file a complaint-" the officer started, when Rosalia walked in "Hey, Sara!" her cheerful voice cut through. Sara turned to her, her eyebrows softened, "You're here", she murmured, weakly smiling. "What's wrong? Why did you come here? Is everything ok?" Rosalia saw the scared look on Sara's face. "It's just-" Sara started, she was shaking in fear. Rosalia walked to her, "Sara? Is everything ok?"

"No…I think someone is stalking me, it might be too early to say so, but I don't know, I just wanted to tell you," Sara said, waiting for a reply. "Stalking? What? What were the signs?"

"Well, first I got this box. It had pictures of me, taken from the hospital, one in the basement, one when I'm working, and there were three others, and there was this note…"

"What did it say?"

"It said I have to watch out, and that I'll pay for something I did"

Rosalia leaned on the desk, her dark green eyes wandering up to the ceiling. "Pay for what you did?" she repeated "Must be one of your patients then" Sara looked confused "My patient? Why would they?" Rosalia sighed as she stepped forward. "Consider this, it could be a family member or a friend of a patient who you were unable to treat or resuscitate, they might be projecting their grief on you, seeking revenge, does that make sense?"

Sara nodded. "Yes." It did make a twisted kind of sense. She lost a lot of her patients. Some of their family or friends had even gotten angry at her; they had thrown stuff, cursed at her because she couldn't save them. They didn't know that every time Sara lost a patient, she lost a little bit of *herself.*

Rosalia cleared her throat "*Sara?*"

Sara looked up, "Oh, sorry…I was just thinking about-" her eyes wandered to the glass window behind Rosalia. Someone was standing, staring right at her. The person had a mask on, black pants, and a black jacket. Sara's eyes widened. She stepped back. "Sara?" Rosalia asked, looking at her. Sara wasn't listening; she stared right at the glass window. "Sara, and also, we cannot initiate an investigation yet, unless you have solid proof, ok? But if anything happens, tell me…even the smallest thing, it may all just be a big prank, but just to be sure, your apartment must have CCTV, am I right?"

Sara wasn't listening; she was looking at the person, it was the stalker, right?

It was, wasn't it? It had to be. No, she did not know for sure. Maybe it was just some homeless person, she blinked away her fear. Sara nodded and turned to Rosalia. "Sara, I asked if your apartment had CCTV, did it?" Rosalia asked again, "Yes, yes, yes, it does", she said, watching the person behind the glass walk away. But wait. They dropped something, a paper, was it? Sara squinted, trying to see, but it fell to the ground. She turned to Rosalia, "I'll call you or come here if anything else happens. I just wanted to make sure you knew, in case something happened to me-" Rosalia nodded "Sure, Sara, I'm always there"

Sara smiled and stepped outside, she walked to the big window outside where the person was standing. She looked down. A business card? Is that what the person dropped? She lifted it.

Pine View Motel

Escape to tranquillity at Pine View Motel, where nature meets comfort. Nestled among the cosy crimson woods, our rooms offer a perfect retreat for relaxation.

Call 90-23-78-73 to book a room, or email pineviewmotelhastings@mail.com

Cash and card accepted, no online payments.

Sara read the business card. "Pine view motel…" she said under her breath. Her eyes wandered to the street as she tried to look for the person who dropped it.

Pine View Motel. *Crimson woods*.

Sara's eyes closed tightly as the memories of the night flooded her mind. The night of the accident. *Two decades ago*. The air had been thick with fog, and Sara remembered the car tumoring over and turning over. The sound of shattering glass and metal grinding against the asphalt road had filled her ears. Her mind was foggy and she lost consciousness. When she woke up in the hospital, her parents were dead, and *Sanya*…she ran away into the woods. Sara still didn't understand why she ran off; maybe she was scared. The police gave up the search for Sanya in 2008, three years after she ran away. They stated they searched every nook and cranny of the woods she ran into, but they didn't find her. They said there was no way she would be alive.

Sara wiped her eyes as she tried to push away the thoughts. Her mind was reeling, she put the business card in her pocket and walked to her car to go back home. She got in her car and put the keys in; her palms were sweaty as she grabbed the steering wheel. She tried calling the number on the card, but it was an automated message.

She didn't go home. She drove to Pine View Motel, even though Sara didn't know why; it just happened, she put the location in on her phone, and she drove. For three hours straight, until she reached a small town near Hastings, Juniper Ridge. The town where the accident happened. The town, which was connected to the woods Sanya disappeared in. Maybe, just maybe, she was still in there?

No, no way.

A small voice in Sara's head said. She didn't want hope. She lost it a long time ago. She parked her car at the small parking lot behind Pine View Motel. There was just a small red sedan parked at the end. The hair behind Sara's neck stood up as she stepped out of her car The cold autumn wind blew on her face, she grabbed her purse and walked towards the Motel. It wasn't very old, but not very new either. The walls on the outside were painted a deep coat of red, and paint was peeling off, and there was a huge sign on top. The doors were a deep shade of brown, and a wooden sign swung gently in the breeze, making a creaking sound. Sara opened the door and stepped in. A small lady was sitting behind the check - in desk, her legs on the table, she was chewing gum in a weird way, and speaking loudly on the phone. Her eyes landed on Sara, and she hung up on the call.

"Check in?" She asked in a heavy accent, as she spun the gum around in her mouth. Her feet were still up on the table. Sara gulped. Should she check in? I mean, it wasn't safe, right? She had nothing on her, except her phone and some cash, and she was far away from the city. And even worse, the woods, well, crimson woods, were right behind this motel, and it creeped her out. She had never been this close to the place where the accident happened. "Are you gonna say something, dear?" The lady asked, snapping her fingers at Sara. "Oh, um, yes, I'd like to book a room for one, please, just for one night"

The lady nodded and put her feet down as she took a book out of the drawer. "Sign here, put your name in, and number", she pushed a book across the desk to Sara, handing her a pen. Sara grabbed it and filled it in, and handed it back. The lady sighed and got up, still aggressively chewing the gum and turned her back as she grabbed keys from a wall, where all the keys were hung. "Room 5, it's to your left", she handed the keys, her long nails scratching against Sara's palms. Sara looked down the hallways, realising her room would face the woods, and there was probably a window which had a view of them. "Is it possible if I get a room on the other side, without the view of the woods?"

The lady snickers, "Why, scared of the woods when it's dark?" she asked, smirking.

“No, I just”, Sara started, “Well, if you ain't scared then go in.” The lady put her feet back up on the table and took her phone out. Sara sighed and walked to the room. The hallways were dark and dimly lit. She walked in front of room 5, her hands clutching onto the keys tightly. She put them in the keyhole and twisted the keys. She walked in as she locked the door behind her. The room was dark, and it had a window next to the bed, with a view of the woods. Sara gulped. “Great… I have a view of the woods where my sister went missing years ago, perfect, isn’t it? Why? Why am I even here?” She closed the curtains and lay down on the bed, still in her flannel shirt and jeans. Her eyes shot up to the ceiling, where there was black mould growing. “Oh god, if I’m in here for long enough, I’ll die”, she mumbled, getting up. Wait. Why was she here? Oh, right, she found the business card, her alleged stalker dropped, and her dumb self-decided to go exactly there, why, why? She asked herself. Her mind raced as she stood in front of the mirror. “I should ask the lady in front if someone else booked a room here”, she rolled her eyes. That lady would be of no help, but she had to try. She walked out and towards the front desk. “Excuse me?” She said, the lady turned, she was on her phone again. “What?” She asked, still on the phone. “I was wondering…”

“Wondering what?” The lady snapped. “Do people check in here a lot, or is it?” Sara asked, but the lady interrupted “, Why do you want to know?”

“Just curious,” Sara mumbled. The lady huffed as she hung up on her phone. “Ok, lady, I don’t know who you are, but if you can't tell, there is no one here, except you and someone else"

"Who else?" Sara asked as she walked towards the front desk. The lady looked up and scrunched her nose, the wrinkles on her forehead darkened, "I don't know, that person had booked an appointment over the phone, and just walked in and took the keys"

Sara nodded, "Thank you." She stepped outside of the motel, as she watched it get darker outside, her head was hurting. She stared at the red sedan parked a couple of slots away from her car. She walked towards it, and when she noticed something on her car, "What?" She whispered as she walked to her car. There was another box. "Oh my god", she took the box and tore it open. Another note.

You're not very smart, are you? Going to a motel in the middle of nowhere? What if I tell you that I was the person who dropped it? I dropped it on purpose. I knew you would come here, Sara.

Oh no. Oh no. Oh no. Sara ran back to the motel, leaving the note there. She dashed past the front desk and to her room. She patted her pockets as she took her keys out and went into her room. She grabbed her purse and ran out, leaving the keys still dangling from the door. The lady at the front desk looked up from her phone "Where are you going? Lady?" she called, but Sara ran outside, grabbed her car keys and got in. She pressed the pedal and tried to start her car. The engine made a sound. "What?" She mumbled, looking at the front of her car.

She stepped out quickly and lifted the hood of the car. There was another note.

If you came here, you might as well stay.

No. No, no. Sara got back in the car and punched the steering wheel. She tried to start the car again, but it wouldn't turn on. She leaned back in her seat and held her forehead, as beads of sweat ran down them. What should she do? She grabbed her phone and called Rosalia.

Thank god there was cell service.

“Hello?” Sara heard from her phone; she sighed, closing her eyes in relief. “Rosalia, you need to help me”, Sara whispered, her voice trembling

“What happened? Where are you?”

Sara gulped as she held onto the phone tightly, “I’m in Juniper Ridge.”

“What? Juniper Ridge? You mean the one near.” Rosalia's voice cracked through the phone

“Hastings. Yes.”

“What are you doing there?”

“The…The person I saw through the window in the police station dropped something as they left, and I went and took it. It was a business card for Pine View Motel, and I don't know why, but I drove here.”

“I’m coming there. Right now, what was the motel's name again?”

“Pine View Motel.”

"Oh my god, Sara, why did you even drive there all by yourself, when you know you have a freaking stalker?"

Sara didn't reply, she heard Rosalia's car start, and she clung onto the phone. "I'll try to drive and come as soon as I can, even though Hastings is almost three hours away…I have informed the police there. God, Sara, why did you do this?" Rosalia said after a few minutes.

"Just come fast, please, I'm scared"

"I'll be there, okay?"

"Thank you", Sara sighed, "Go back into the motel, Sara, book a room if you have to."

"I already did"

"Then go back in, you're outside in a car, it's not safe."

Sara slowly stepped out of the car, and as she held her purse, she looked around. The wind was cold, and the trees looked creepy. The only thing she heard was the rustling of the leaves and the signboard creaking, she slipped the car keys into her pocket and ran back to the motel. She went back to her room, which she had left open, she closed the door and locked it, and sat on a chair. "I'm in my room now", she updated her. Rosalia nodded to herself and said, "Stay there, I'll be there in three hours, well, there isn't much traffic out here, I'll be there faster." Sara leaned back in the wooden chair. She put the phone on speaker and placed it on the bed next to her. Sara could hear Rosalia driving and the car sounds. She held her head in her palms when she heard a rustle. Sara looked up, her eyes were wide and red, she looked around as she grabbed her phone, and she peeked near the door. No one. “What…” she whispered as she leaned back. There, she heard it again. “Oh my god, what is that?” she said, looking around, her heart pounding in her chest. “What? Sara, did you say something?” Rosalia asked from the phone, her voice cracking. “I thought I heard something,” Sara whispered, as she bent down to look under the bed.

Nothing.

She sighed, “Rosalia, maybe I should go to the.” She heard a crash, she turned her head towards the window, about five feet away from the chair she was sitting on, and there was glass on the floor. It happened so fast, Sara screamed as she jumped back on the bed. “SARA? WHAT HAPPENED?” Rosalia shouted. Sara was too scared to even speak; she was shaking as she gripped onto the bed sheets. She couldn’t see what or who broke the window, because she had closed the curtains. She expected someone to jump in through the window and kill her. But no one came in.

Time stood still for a minute, it felt like an hour for Sara, as she stared at the window with closed curtains and glass on the floor, Rosalia was shouting for Sara through the phone, but Sara couldn't speak, she gulped and slowly got up and walked to the window, her hands trembling, her shoes squeaked against the dark wooden floors, “please, please, please” she whispered as she stopped in front of the windows, and took a deep breath. She yanked the curtains open and stood frozen. No one. Just the dark, deep woods were in front of her, and a broken window, and glass piercing through her shoes. The wind blew through the windows, and hit her face, her hair blew back, and her eyes closed as dirt flew into them. Sara could still hear Rosalia's panicked voice on the call. But she wasn't paying attention. She saw another note. Right there, placed on the windowsill. She grabbed the note.

If you want to see her, go in.

What? Sara held the note close and read it again. There was only one person it could be. *Sanya. Sanya Singh*, her sister, who went missing in the woods twenty years ago. Sara gulped; she had to go. It was her sister; she might be in trouble, and-

No. No. It was dumb. Why would Sanya still be alive? Someone would have seen her; it's not like Crimson Woods is huge, people go hunting there all the time. This was a trick to lure me in.

Sara stepped back from the windows. She felt the glass in her shoe go into her foot "Ouch-" She was going to bend down to her foot when she saw something. Deep in the woods. A pair of eyes. Sanya? They stared back at Sara until they turned and ran off into the forest. It could be Sanya? It had to be. Something in Sara's mind clicked. Sara jumped out of the window and ran. She ran into the forest, her foot was bleeding, as she felt the glass go deeper inside her flesh with every step she took. She didn't understand why she was running; it was like those eyes lured her, they cast a spell on Sara, like a siren does with her voice. Sara felt her feet burn as she stepped on dry leaves and heard them crunch under her weight. The forest air was thick with the earthy scent of damp soil and decaying leaves. She stumbled and fell forward, a cry escaping her lips. Her knees scraped against the forest floor, and her fingernails dug into the dirt. She looked forward, and she couldn't see anyone. She got up and leaned on a tree. "What did I do?" she whispered as she held her foot in pain. "Why did I just run into the-" she stopped. She heard some more leaves crunching behind her. She slowly turned back, "Sanya?" she whispered. Another pair of eyes was staring at her. Green eyes. "You're not-" she stumbled back. "Who are you?"

The voice was deep; it was a man. "The one who left you those notes."

Sara tried to see the man's face, but it was dark; she only saw his eyes. Rosalia should be here by now, right? She would have alerted the police at Hastings. Sara would be fine. "What do you want?" Sara managed to say, as she tried to hold back tears of pain. The glass was completely in her foot now.

The man laughed.

"What do you want?" Sara asked, "Who are you?"

"Stay quiet, now, we don't want you getting caught, do we?" The man said, his voice cracking. "What?" Sara stuttered.

"I said quite"

"No…No, I can't, oh my god, I'm stupid, why did I even think?" Sara screamed, as she fell to the floor, she was crying in pain, she felt like her foot would fall off. She had to go to the hospital, or she would lose blood and die. Sara heard police cars, far away, near the motel. The

Hastings police must have been alerted; they were here. Sara got up and held onto the tree. “They will find me”, she said, as she fell onto the tree, her leg giving way. “Oh no, they won't,” The man said, laughing.

“What, they will-”

“Run”

“What?”

“Run deeper into the woods, Sara. Or I will shoot you” The man pulled out something. Sara couldn't see, but it was a gun; she heard him load the bullets. She had to run back to the motel, but he was telling her to run into the forest. “I can’t my leg-”

“Run”

Sara heard him lift the gun up. So she ran. She ran deeper into the forest, her foot was bleeding, leaving bloody footprints, and her bloody shoe fell off as she ran. She had hoped the police would find her because of the blood; she pressed her foot harder into the ground so they would leave traces. The shadows danced around her, her breath came in ragged gasps, each inhale stung her dry throat, her palms scraped against the rough bark of a tree, and she looked back to see if the man was there. He wasn’t. But she didn’t stop running. She ran, until she couldn't, the ground was blurring beneath her, she felt her knees weaken, and her forehead broke out in cold sweat, her foot was killing her, and her eyes flashed as she fell onto the moist forest floor, her head hit a tree trunk and she tasted blood in her mouth, the forest sounds faded away, as she closed her eyes and passed out.

Chapter – 3

11:13 pm

Rosalia slammed her car door and ran to the motel. She saw three police cars parked outside the motel, she barged into the front lobby and saw a police officer taking a statement from the lady at the front desk. "She also wanted a room without a view of the forest", the lady said, as she chewed on her gum, unfazed at the situation. Rosalia rolled her eyes and walked up to the officer. "Which room is it?" she asked

"Down there, Ma'am," The officer pointed at the hallway. Other officers were standing. She rushed to the room, her feet echoing against the wooden floors, "Did you find her?" she asked as she went into the room. She saw the window broken, and Sara's pink purse lying on the bed; her phone was also there, still turned on. "We got a 19-12 on Sara Singh, I repeat, a 19-12, yes, over", an officer said to his radio. Sara had run into the woods, where her stalker might have been. "Are there cameras around here?" Rosalia asked

"No, officer, none, it's an old motel off the highway, why would there be any cameras around here?" An officer said as he walked into the room holding a notepad. Rosalia let out a deep sigh as she held her temples, "Exactly, it's an old motel off the highway, you *need* cameras."

"Why did she just run into the forest like that?" Rosalia asked, holding her head with her cold palms, "She knew she had a stalker…she wouldn't have run in unless…unless someone either broke in and took her, or they called her in, but I don't think she would just go in."

"Maybe they had a weapon and forced her to follow them in?" an officer asked. Rosalia nodded, "Maybe…are there officers in there searching?"

"Yes, officer, they are, right now."

"I'm going in, get me that torch."

"I think they have enough-"

I said, "Get me that torch."

The officer grabs a torch and hands it to Rosalia. She snatches it and walks out of the motel, into the open. The fresh night air hits her face, as her heavy police boots thud through the ground, she reaches the entry of the forest, where a police officer is closing the entry off. Rosalia walks towards him, "Let me through, I need to go-" the officer looks at Rosalia's badge, as it shines in the moonlight. He nods and makes way for her. She turns on her flashlight and points it to the ground. She hears other officers speaking in the distance, and she follows the sound. Her heavy boots echo through the night as she reaches some officers. "Do you know where she went?" she asked, stopping near the officers.

"Ma'am, she went back."

"What?" Rosalia's eyebrows shot up as she leaned forward.

“She ran back, she went into the forest, then she ran back outside”, another officer said.

“That makes no sense, we would have seen her, she couldn’t have run off that fast…and I was on a call with her, I heard her scream after I heard the window break, then she said nothing and I heard nothing, it still makes zero sense on why she would run into the forest and run back out” Rosalia said, turning her flashlight off.

“We saw some footprints, and one of the footprints had blood on it”, explained an officer. “Must have been the glass at the window in her room.” The officer nods, “Maybe, the footprints stop all of a sudden, and it looks like she walked back, see for yourself.” The officer shines his torchlight at the ground, showing the footprints.

Rosalia sighs. This is more complicated than she thought. She pulled her hair away from her face as she zipped her jacket up. “So, she ran in and ran back out?”

“Yes, we know for sure she did not go deeper into the woods,” he said, turning his flashlight towards the trees.

“Ok, if you say so,” Rosalia huffed, a cool breeze hitting the back of her neck

Chapter – 4

1:05 am

Sara did not run back. She was lying on the floor of the forest, her head bleeding, and her foot throbbing.

The stalker, or whomever he was, was smart, you could say, he was *experienced*, he removed the bloody footprints by covering it up with mud and leaves, and he knew it was going to rain, and the Hastings police weren't going to search that deep for a missing persons case, he made it look like Sara ran back out by using her shoe that fell off. Thank god for that shoe, or else he would have to go find her in the woods and take it. He knew she wouldn't make it far, but she would make it far enough so the police wouldn't hear her whimper or shout in pain. The stalker had climbed up a tree and was waiting as the police left the scene. He smiled as the last police officer grabbed his torch and walked away. His plan worked. Now the police were certain she had run back and was probably in some town. The stalker slowly got down the tree, his black leather boots scratching against the tree's bark as he jumped down. He grabbed his side bag and walked deep into the woods, looking for Sara.

Sara was still there, her head still bleeding from hitting the forest floor. She slowly opened her eyes and held her head as blood ran down her hands and into her hair. She brushed her hand against her forehead, as she felt the warm, sticky blood stick to her head. She sat up and leaned against a tree. Her flannel shirt was soaked with blood, and it stuck to her skin; she felt mud going inside the wound on her foot. "Oh my god, where's my shoe?" She leaned down and held her leg. She felt the glass in her flesh, as thick, warm blood trickled down from it. The air was heavy with the metallic smell of blood filling the air around her. With trembling hands, she pushed herself off the forest floor and stood up and looked around. Where were the police? Where was Rosalia?

She heard someone. She knew it wasn't the police; it was the same heavy footsteps she had heard. She clasped her hand against her mouth and hid behind the tree. She stopped breathing as she tried not to make a sound. She peeked and saw a man. The same man. His light eyes shone in the moonlight. She saw his black leather boots and a bag around his side. He walked around trying to find her; she knew it. He walked past her. But he stopped. He felt something stick to his boots. He bent down and took out his flashlight, he shone the light on his shoe. Bright red.

Blood.

He laughed and shone the torch to the forest floor. He saw blood on the ground and blood on a tree. He slowly walked to the tree and then behind it. He saw Sara, closing her eyes, and her hands clasped against her mouth; she was crying. He laughed; she was so dumb. Sara opened her eyes slowly as she looked at the man.

"Pl-please, ju-just", she tried to say. The man grabbed a needle from his bag and slammed it into her arm. She fell back, the needle still in her arm, she pulled it out, but it was too late, "Wh-what is that-" she whispered, holding her arm in pain, she was too weak to fight back. "Something that will keep you asleep for a while," the man replied. Sara felt her eyes blur. She rubbed them, "Why are you doing this?" she asked, trying to stay awake.

"You'll pay for what?"

Sara didn't hear him; she fell asleep as the contents in the needle entered her blood.

The man dragged her across the forest floor to a car, he lifted her and threw her in the trunk and slammed it shut. He walked up to the front and started the car.

4:36 am

Sara heard the rumbling of an engine and rustling of leaves. She opened her eyes, but it was like her eyes were still closed. She put her hands to her face and rubbed them; she felt blood trickle into her eyes. "Where am I?" she mumbled as she tried to sit up, but she hit her head on something. "No…I can't be," she felt around. She heard the engine. She started to cry as she tried to find something to break out. Her hair caught onto some plastic on the car, and it ripped her hair off. She winced in pain, and she banged against the back of the trunk, trying to open it. She cried, and cried, and cried. She was going to die.

She fainted from pain, fear, and exhaustion.

6:00 am

Sara woke up in a start, her hands and legs were tied, she felt the rope digging into her wrists and ankles, she saw her foot was wrapped with a cloth, but she saw blood seeping into the fabric, she looked around, she was in a small, dirty room, there were no windows, but she could hear birds chirping outside, and other forest sounds. The room walls were painted a dark shade of brown, and it had a moist smell; the air was thick, with a musty odour. She saw buckets of bleach and paint around her. Her head was throbbing, and she wiggled around in the chair she was tied to. The chair creaked under her weight, and a tear ran down her face. She didn't have anything around her mouth. Even if she were to scream, who would hear her in this forest?

Sara's head hung down as a teardrop fell from her cheek to her jeans, which were torn. She smelt dried blood, her eyes scattered around the room as she tried to wriggle the chair to the door, but she was too tired, her foot hurt, her head was bleeding, and she was just exhausted.

The stalker knew that.

The clouds above the forest thickened, swirling together. Just moments before the sun had risen and sent a golden light through the forest, but the warmth was gone. A low rumble of thunder echoed through the forest. Sara closed her eyes as she heard rain drumming against the roof of the small room she was in. Sara's eyes welled up in tears as she realised the only bloody footprints she had left would have been washed away by now. She felt drops of water hit the top of her head from a crack in the roof, which washed the blood from her hair down to her face, as blood dripped onto her face. She winced in pain as a drop of water fell into an open wound in her head.

6:56 am

Rosalia stood outside the Hastings police station, as she explained the search plan, she decided to take the lead on the case. She laid out a map she had drawn so she could explain the search plan to the officers. "Ok, everyone, I need you guys to listen up", Rosalia called, as everyone gathered around her table and looked at the map. "The circle over there is where we found Sara's footprints, and then we saw that she ran back outside, am I right?" The officers nodded. "Right, so we have searched the area, and it's clear, now we need to search the areas I have shaded in red, those are the key places she might have run too, we must also search in other motels, restaurants, petrol bunks and any other place in Juniper ridge, put up missing posters both in Juniper Ridge and in Hastings. We must search the small roads that disconnect from the main road between Hastings and Juniper Ridge as well. But for now, our main priority will be these places," Rosalia points to the shaded areas. "We still have time, I'm sure Sara has not gone that far."

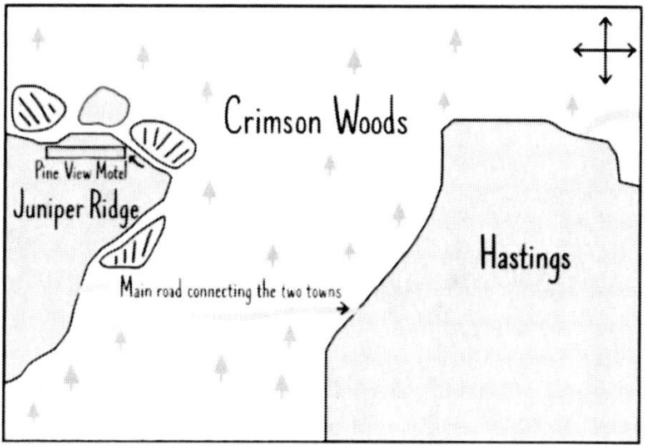

An officer leaned away from the table. She looked at Rosalia, "But why did Sara run off like that? It has to do something regarding the stalker, right? Maybe she saw him when she ran into the woods, got scared and ran back out…" Rosalia shrugged, "Maybe, we can't be sure until we find some clues or evidence. The stalker might have even taken Sara away" Her voice cracked, as she held back tears. She couldn't let anything happen to Sara. She had saved her son's life when he was sick. "We have to find her. Come on now, I made a list of who is searching where, and I have sent it to all of your phones. Partner up and let's get going," Rosalia clapped her hands. "I want everyone to report back here at exactly 10:30 am. Anything you find, get it back, make note of any unusual footprints or items, keep your eyes peeled, and your ears open, interrogate the locals, ask if they saw her, or anything weird." The officers nodded as they left. Rosalia sighed and grabbed her radio, and walked out. She had to find Sara.

Chapter – 5

In their mind, you ruined everything — so they'll ruin what you love the most.

The stalker stepped out of the police station he smirked, straightened his badge and walked out. The stalker was a police officer.

Officer William Burt.

He got into his police car and started the engine. Still smiling, he took off to Pine View Motel, where everyone would start their search. "Rosalia is dumber than I thought," he scoffed as he turned on the radio.

He leaned back in his seat as he drove. He was glad that the search being conducted was not even anywhere close to where Sara really was. She was hidden deep in the woods, and the places Rosalia marked as "main priority" were completely wrong. Officer William was smart…and he knew it. He parked his car near the entrance of Pine View Motel and stepped out, and waved to some other officers. Officer Cho walked up to him, "Where are you assigned to search?" William asked. "Oh, I was assigned the south."

"Right…" William nodded and walked away. The morning air was fresh. He grabbed his torchlight and started walking into the forest. "Do you need a partner, officer?" Someone called from behind. "No."

He walked deeper into the forest, shining his flashlight through the wet ground. He walked away from the assigned spot and went north. He walked in silence, only the heavy leather boots crunching against the leaves and twigs making sounds. He walked for two hours until he stopped. He pulled another set of car keys from his pocket and walked over to a tree. His other car was parked there. He got in and put his mask on, and a leather, black jacket, and he started driving through the forest.

9:30 am

Sara drifted in and out of consciousness. She woke up again because of her head. It hurt a lot; she felt blood streaming down her face and into her mouth. She spat the blood out and sighed as she shivered in the cold. The rain had stopped, and she felt cold. Her mind was racing. Was she going to die here? She couldn't. And where were the police? Where was Rosalia?

Sara tried to break free from the rope, but it was too tight. She tried to move the chair backwards, or somewhere, she had to escape. She wriggled her chair to a wall with a vent on the bottom, and she rubbed her ankles with a rope tied around them on it. She felt her skin burn, but it didn't work. She cried in pain as she hung her head in front of her. The tears blurred her vision as she cried softly. She could taste blood in her mouth. Her ears were ringing when they suddenly heard something. A rumble. She heard it come closer. It was an engine. "Police?" she whispered in hope, as she stared at the door. She heard the rattling of keys as they unlocked the door, and the door swung open. The same green eyes she saw last night looked at her, the same man who dragged her into this. She scanned his face, but she could only see his eyes and forehead. He was wearing a mask. He had wrinkles on his forehead. Must be older than forty, he was wearing the same black leather boots he was wearing last night. Sara looked at him. “Who are you?” she asked in a weak voice.

William didn’t reply; he grabbed a bag from the side and tossed it at her, a bright red first aid kit peeking out from it. “There are bandages and antiseptics in there. Use them.”

“I’m tied up,” she croaked, her voice barely audible.

“I don't care, figure it out”, William snapped, turned back to slam the door and lock her up again. “Stitches…” Sara whispered. “Huh?” William turned back around. “My foot…it needs stitches,” she said, straightening her back. William rolls his eyes and slams the door. Sara hears him locking her back in. She sighs and leans her head on the chair. She stared at the bag he left, which had first aid. She wiggled her chair towards it, but she fell forward and hit her face. “No-” she heard her nose crack, and she rolled in the chair to the side. She was on the floor, and she felt her nose bleed as it seeped down her mouth and neck. She tried to pull the bag with her tied-up feet, but it wasn’t working. She tried to sit back up, but she couldn’t. She felt blood oozing from her head, pooling beneath her, and she felt the rope scratching her ankles, cutting deep into her flesh. She closed her eyes.

What if this is it?

She heard the man start his car and leave.

She lay on the cold floor, still tied up, her face pressed against the rough surface. With a deep breath, she opened her eyes, the sharp stinging in her head and pain in her foot hitting her. She stared at the first aid kit. She dropped her shoulder and arched her back as she rolled against the floor. She felt the rope get tighter around her wrists, and the chair creaked as she put all her body weight on it she to roll over again. She repeated it.

Roll.

Stop.

Roll.

Stop.

Roll.

Stop.

Roll.

Stop.

Roll.

Stop.

She was near the bag, she reached out for the handles with her mouth and grabbed them with her teeth. She saw the white fabric on the handles turn red from the blood in her mouth. She bit down on the hard plastic of the first aid kit, her teeth sunk into it and she dragged it out of the bag, she tried to pull the latch, but her jaw hurt, she saw blood trickle down from her teeth, but she strained her neck and bit harder as she tried to open the latch, with a desperate tug, the latch clicked open, and she felt he first aid kit open, she twisted her body awkwardly as she stared at the items in the box. Bingo, some first aid scissors, they were small, not very sharp, but it would have to do, she grabbed them with her mouth and put it on the floor, she dragged herself against the floor and turned around and rolled until her hands were near the scissors, she felt around the cold floor until she felt metal, she grabbed the scissors and sliced them against the rope, with one last slice, she felt the blades go into her flesh with each thrust of the blade, but now her hands were free, she brought her hands up to her face and wiped the blood and sweat away. She used her hands to sit up and untie the ropes around her ankles. She sighed in relief as she bent down and grabbed bandages to wrap her foot and head, with shaking hands she applied antiseptic on her foot, as it burned against her skin, she wrapped her swollen wrist in bandages and stood up, she put the scissors in her pocket and grabbed the bag and put it around her, she ran to the door and tried to open it, but it was locked, she dug through the first aid kit and found a pin. “I hope this works”, she muttered under her breath as she inserted the pin into the keyhole. Her ears were ringing, and she stood in front of the door, fidgeting with the pin as she tried to open the door. “There’s no way this will work”, she mumbled. She jammed the pin into the keyhole and shook it. *Click.* What was that? Was it the lock? Sara slowly pushed the door open, half expecting it not to be unlocked, but it was. She saw the forest in front of her, and a small smile crossed her face. She stepped out and looked around. *Saved.* She still had her watch; she checked the time.

12:32 pm

William had to practically run out of the forest after parking his “secret” car in the forest. He had to make sure Sara didn't die. *Yet.* He gave her the first aid kit. He ran to his police car parked near Pine View Motel and drove it back to the police station.

He was supposed to report back 2 hours ago. Officer Rosalia asked them to come at 10:30 am. He rushed out of his car as he parked it in front of the police station. He saw officers leaving, so he ran inside. Rosalia was standing in the middle, talking to other officers, her eyes fell on William. “You're late,” she said. “Sorry, lost track of time in the woods”, William said, trying to catch his breath. “And that's why you have a watch.” Rosalia snapped.

William nodded, looking down. Rosalia put her hand up against the wall. She sighed.

2 pm

Sara didn't stop running. She ran, she didn't know whether she was going deeper into the forest or escaping it. She just had to get as far away as she could from the cabin, or whatever it was she was locked in. Sara felt the hot sun hit her back as she ran between trees. Her heart was pounding, and her face was sweaty. She felt the bandages around her foot loosen and peel off, but she didn't stop running. She felt her hair get caught on branches as they ripped it out. She didn't look back, even though she knew the stalker wasn't there. She just had to run. Sara stumbled to a halt, as she fell on her knees, she gasped for air, as she held her chest. Every time she took a breath, it felt like she was swallowing fire. She leaned against rough tree bark, as it dug into her back. Sweat rolled down her forehead, dripping into her eyes. She wiped her brow with shaky hands. With shaking legs, she pushed herself off the forest floor and limped to the side. She peeled off the bandage on her foot and pulled out another one from the bag she took with her. She wrapped it around her foot as she peeled off the dry blood from the sides. With a deep shuddering breath, she stood up straight, every muscle in her screaming in protest. She slowly walked as she held onto the trees for support. She had to get out of the woods. She saw clouds cover the sky, and thunder rumbled. "Great. It's going to rain again," She mumbled, annoyed. She made her way through the forest in pain.

4:47 pm

Rosalia had sent the police for another search an hour ago. She was searching the south side of Crimson Woods. Her heart was racing as she kicked leaves of her path. There were two other officers with her. She felt raindrops fall on her; she sighed. If there was any evidence, the rain would wash it away. Her boots stopped crunching against the leaves as the rain moistened them; she felt the rain get heavier. She put her hand above her forehead as she scanned the forest floor. The other two officers turned back. "Maybe we should get going, ma'am, it's going to get dark soon-" "Right." Rosalia nodded. She watched the officers turn back and walk behind her. She turned back and watched them leave. She felt the rain pound against her back. Her eyes welled up in tears. What if Sara were never found? They had been searching for hours, but they still had no clue where she went. Rosalia felt herself falling as she cried, her hands dug deep into the forest floor. "Where are you, *Sara*?" she whispered, crying.

Chapter – 6

When people go missing in forests, the general narrative suggests they either get lost and die of exposure, fall into hazards, or their remains are found later, with some attributing it to natural causes or even fabricated stories.

Sara blinked her eyes open. She hadn't meant to fall asleep; exhaustion overpowered her. It stopped raining, but it was dark now, hard to tell the time, maybe around 8 or 9 pm. She stood up, her knees weak; she had to get out of here. She walked, following the moonlight as it seeped through the tall trees. Forest sounds were ringing in her ears. She saw a small pond in the distance, as the moonlight reflected off its surface, her eyes glimmered, and her lips curled into a smile as she ran to it, falling to her feet as she bent down next to it, she cupped her palms and dipped them into the water, she drank it. "Eugh", she spat it out. "Not drinkable", she murmured. With a sigh, she took her bag off and put her feet into the water. As she cleaned them, she washed her face, arms and hair. She stared at her reflection in the water; her face had scars, and her hair was knotted and ripped. She sat at the edge of the pond, staring into the sky. She felt calm, but it wasn't a pleasant feeling of calmness; she knew if she didn't get out of here, she would die, either from dehydration or some wild animal. *Or…the stalker.*

10:55 pm

William rushed out of the police station; his shift was over, but he wasn't going home; he had to check on Sara in the woods. He rushed to the forest, but he entered from another side. He knew the search for Sara was still going on near Pine View Motel, so he drove his car to the other side and parked it. He walked into the woods, his torchlight shining through the darkness, and he made his way to his hidden car, tucked behind trees, and got in and started driving.

The car headlights shone through the dark forest. The car came to a stop in front of the room. He sighed and got down, grabbing a bag of food. He walked to the door and pulled out his keys. He shone the torchlight on the door. "*NO...NO... NO,*" he dropped the torch as he saw the already opened door, he kicked it open and shone his torch light in the dark room. She was gone. Sara escaped. "She took the freaking medical bag. She took it." He slapped his forehead, "I must have left a pin or needle in it, *oh my god, I'm stupid, oh no, no, no.*" He slammed the room door closed and ran to his car he started the engine and drove into the forest. She still had to be out there.

No one could survive a night in the woods.

12 am

Rosalia returned from the search, still no luck. It has been a day since she went missing. Not a single clue on where Sara was. She walked into the police station as she threw the car keys aside. She grabbed the map and stared at it. What if-

What if Sara didn't go out? What if the footprints were planted? It was rare, but there could be a chance? Right?

Rosalia got up she sent a text to the other officers. "*New search plan. Let's discuss it tomorrow, at seven am.*" Rosalia grabbed her map and started tracing which places they were going to cover. Her heart raced as she circled parts of the forest, assigning them to different officers.

1:07 am

William parked his car, the engine's hum fading into the stillness of the woods. He had been searching for hours, shining his bright headlights through the woods. Where had she gone? He stepped out of his car and made his way to a small cabin he had built. His home. He built his home in Crimson Woods. It was his sanctuary, his refuge from the chaos. He unlocked the door and stepped in. Of course, it was far from the room he had locked Sara in. He closed the door behind him and turned on the lights. He took his jacket off and hung it behind the wooden door. He sat down on his couch and put his feet up on the table. He sighed in relaxation as he leaned back on his couch. He wasn't *too* worried about Sara escaping. He knew the woods like the back of his hand. He lived in the woods all his life, even as a little boy, with his parents.

He gulped. He would find Sara. He knew it.

Chapter – 7

She had been missing for a day now.

6 am

Sara woke up as the sun rays hit her through the trees. She sat up and rubbed her eyes. The forest was alive with sounds. She took a deep breath and scanned her surroundings as she sat up. She looked down at her cracked watch; it had been a day since she had gone missing. She had to get out of this place. The air was cool, and she knew it would rain again. She heard something. A trickle of a stream? She walked past the edge of the pond where she had fallen asleep, her clothes were damp and soggy as they clung to her skin. She saw a small stream passing through the forest floor, and her eyes lit up. Fresh water. Sara hurried to the stream, she knelt beside it and cupped her hands as she brought fresh, cold water to her parched mouth. As she drank, she glanced around. She could follow the stream; maybe it would lead her out. After taking a few more sips she stood up as she wiped her dirty hands on her clothes. She stood at the edge of the bank, listening to the gurgling of water.

6:57 am

Rosalia waited in the station as she saw officers come in. She had a new plan. She watched the last few officers come in as she shut the door. "Right…so new plan, everyone", she said, clapping her hands to get everyone's attention. "We are going to search the whole forest," she said, looking up from the table. "What?" an officer said, "But, I thought Sara ran back out, it's a waste of time and resources if we search the *whole* forest. Crimson Woods is not that small, you know."

Rosalia tried to speak up, but she was interrupted. "Yeah, you don't know, officer, you're not from here, it's going to take us weeks if we have to look through all of the Crimson woods."

Rosalia took a deep breath as she scanned the officers in front of her, "We can't dismiss the possibility that Sara might still be out there in the woods."

One officer, visibly annoyed, crossed his arms "But the evidence we found, the footprints, indicate she exited the forest; we don't have a solid lead that she is still in the forest." Other officers nod in agreement. Rosalia rolled her eyes, "I have a doubt…what if those footprints were planted, to confuse us?" We can't overlook any possibility, officer."

"Look, officer, it's a small town, and a huge forest, you don't really know much about it, since you're not from here, we should focus on the evidence we have, which clearly states Sara exited from Crimson woods," another officer chimed in. Rosalia gripped her pen as she wiped sweat off her forehead. She frowned. "Look, Rosalia, with all due respect, this isn't your call. We need to be smart, not *emotional*. We follow the leads, like stated in protocol," the senior officer said, looking at Rosalia. "*Emotional*? What do you mean by that?"

"We all very well know Sara is your friend, and you want to look for her everywhere, that doesn't mean we look in places that we clearly know she isn't in," the officer said, looking around the room, his arms raised up in defence.

Rosalia's heart sank. Another, police interrupted, "I think Officer William should take the lead on this, he knows the woods like the back of his hand."

Rosalia felt her head and stomach turn, "Wait, what? You can't just."

"Sorry, but we need someone who is actually from here. You're from the city, you don't know this place like some of us do…so, does everyone agree that Officer William takes the lead?" The officer looked at everyone. Everyone nods, and all heads turn to William. He smiles. "Thank you for trusting me with this case. I'll make sure we find Sara and bring her to safety. Let's stick to the plan, search the outskirts of Crimson Woods, not inside. The evidence *clearly* suggests she is not in the woods. His gaze turns to Rosalia. He cleared his throat and continued. "Let's focus on asking people if they saw her, spreading the news, and sticking up missing posters. I'm sure she is in town, it's not too late, let's get going."

Rosalia watched everyone leave the room. She turned to William, her eyes red, "You're making a huge mistake, I think Sara is still in the woods," she muttered, her teeth clenched.

"Officer Rosalia, you can go back to the city now. We will handle it" William nodded as he left. Rosalia clenched her fists as she saw him leave the building.

7:45 am

William got into his car, smiling. He had the lead. He could now just lead the officers away from where Sara really was, in the woods. But he still had to find her. She ran away, she was lost, but he knew he could find her.

He just had to make sure Rosalia would not interfere; everything was going as he had planned. But Rosalia knew something; she knew Sara was still in the woods, William had to be careful. If Rosalia started searching on her own, she would find clues or something he might have missed. He felt his phone vibrate in his pocket, he lifted it up, "Who is it?" Rosalia. He sighed as he cut the call and blocked her.

Rosalia threw her phone across the table. He wasn't picking up the call. She had to tell William to at least search the outskirts of the other side of the woods. At least. The word echoed in her mind as she leaned back in her chair. She grabbed her phone and texted him.

'William, please, search the outskirts of the forest, at least. We might find some clues. I will do it myself, but I could use some help. Please send some officers.'

She clicked send. She got a response.

'This user has blocked you'

Great. He blocked her. She exhaled loudly as she stood up and stared out the window of the police station.

Something was off about William Burt. He was hiding something…Rosalia shook off that feeling.

This wasn't about him. It was about Sara.

8:35 am

Sara was following the stream she found. Her feet were tired as she dragged them across the moist soil. She took small breaks to sip on water from the stream. Her eyes were half closed, she felt the strong wind gush against her face, she stumbled back as her foot slipped on the edge of the stream, she felt her head hit against the rock, and she lost consciousness. The last thing she saw was the sky moving on top of her, as she felt her body flow with the water.

Rosalia had to start the search, even if it was by herself. She grabbed her bag and rushed out of the station as she got into her car. She started driving through Juniper Ridge as she made her way to Pine View Motel. Her car tires screeched against the wet road as she stopped at a gas station. She got down and started filling up the gas. Her eyes wandered around. It was a dark and gloomy morning, with clouds filling the sky. Juniper Ridge had thick air. She got back into her car and started driving. Cold air filled her car as she put the windows down. Her fingers gripped tightly onto the steering wheel, as her knuckles turned white. She took a quick right turn, stopping in front of the motel. She slammed the car door behind her as she started walking into the forest. The mist got thicker as she went deeper. Mud stuck onto her boots as she struggled to walk in the wet forest. Her eyes scanned the trees and the forest floor for any clues, blood, or anything Sara might have left behind.

11 am

"Is that a" Sara stopped walking, her eyes widened, and she stared at the wooden house at the edge of the stream. It looked beautiful, with stained glass windows, lanterns hung around it. She walked towards it, clutching onto her bag. She walked up to the front door and knocked. "Hello? Is anyone there?" She peered through the window. The inside was stunning, there were family portraits on the wall, it was a family of three, parents and a child. Sara smiled softly as she stared at the picture through the window. She turned back to the door and knocked again. "No one must be home", she walked around, feeling a sense of calmness wash over her. She just had to wait here for the family to come back home; she could ask for help. She traced her finger across the wooden walls outside as she wandered around the house. The chirping birds, the gushing water from the stream, the rustling of leaves, all those sounds stopped once she reached the backside of the house. It was almost…empty. She saw the walls behind the house had charred wood on them, almost like they were burnt. It was like a new house was built on an old one. Sara bent down and gazed at the brittle, burnt wood holding up the house. She stared at another door, this one not as pretty as the one in front. She walked towards it and knocked. "Anyone in here?" she asked. Her knuckles turned black as she took her hand away from the door. Ash? Maybe there was a forest fire a couple of months ago, and it burnt down the house, and the family rebuilt this one over it. She knocked again.

She heard something.

Someone?

No, she didn't; her mind was playing tricks on her. She had been out in the elements for a while, trying to escape.

She sighed and stepped back. She sat down, leaning on the door behind her. Sara felt her eyes get heavier as she slowly shut them.

1:06 pm

Rosalia found something. Gauze, or a bandage, was covered in blood. It was stuck to the bark of a tree trunk, and the blood had turned dark brown. She put it in a small plastic bag she had and lifted it to her eyes. Wait… The blood was…brown? That can't be, it had just been a day since Sara had gone missing, it can't be her blood, if it was, that meant it would still be red. She pulled out her phone and googled, *When does blood turn brown?*

She leaned against the tree and started scrolling through her phone, trying to find an answer. She clicked on a site and started reading.

Blood stains: *Everything you need to know*

The time it takes for blood to turn brown, or a shade of darker red, varies based on several factors, including the amount of blood, environmental temperature, humidity, and from which part of the body the blood has come from, ante-mortem or post-mortem.

Blood typically starts to change colour within a few hours, and the browning process can take several days, even up to a week, to fully develop.

Rosalia looked at the bloody gauze again. It was brown. So, it can't be Sara's; it was someone else's. She stuffed the plastic bag in her pocket and started to make her way outside the forest. There had to be *some* connection between it. Right?

Chapter – 8

4:53 pm

Death has a smell. A sickly-sweet odour. It's a distinct smell, something that once you smell, you'll never forget it.

The sickly-sweet odour filled her nostrils as she entered the forensic lab in Hastings, her palms were clammy as she clutched onto the plastic bag. Her eyes wandered around the lab, and she spotted the receptionist. "I'm Officer Rosalia…I had called a few hours ago. I need to test this," she puts the plastic bag up. The receptionist nods and clears his throat, "Go down that way, I'll send in a forensic pathologist." Rosalia walks down the hallways, and sunk into a metal chair, the cold metal touches her bare neck as she leans back, she stares at the plastic bag in her hand, she sighed as she looked away. A tall lady walked to her; her glasses were red and vintage, she had a white lab coat on, and her blonde hair was falling over her face. "Rosalia, right? Here to test a sample?" she asked. Rosalia stood up and extended her hand, "Yes, you must be." The lady took Rosalia's hand and shook it, "I'll be testing the sample. I'm Doctor Iris, forensic pathologist." Rosalia smiled faintly. "Is that the sample?" Iris asked, eyeing the plastic bag. "Yes, yes, it is."

Iris let out a sigh, “Alright, come on”, she started walking, her shoes clicking in the empty hallway. Rosalia followed her. They stopped at the end of the hallway and Iris pushed open a door after scanning her ID. “Come on in,” she exhaled as she sat behind her desk. Rosalia walked in, closing the door behind her. She sat on the blue couch-chair thing in front of Iris and placed the sample in front of her. Iris stared at it, “Before I go to the lab and analyze and test it, I need to know what you exactly want to find out, is it how old the blood is, determine the origin, whose blood it is?” she asked. Rosalia was about to say something, but she interrupted, “When you called about it, I was told it was for a case? Is it murder? Do you think the blood might be a victims or-”

Rosalia shook her head, “No, it is not a murder, it’s a missing person’s case…I think the blood might have *something* to do with.”

“You think the blood is the missing persons or-”

“No. No, Sara, she's the missing person, and she’s been missing for a day now. I read online that blood turns brown after-”

“A week or so, so it’s not Saras then.” Iris cleared her throat, crossing her arms as she leaned back.

Rosalia nodded.

“So, you want me to determine the age of the blood and who it belongs to?”

“As many details as you can get, to help narrow down the suspect”

"So, I'll test it, and send you the reports, also…are you the only officer working on this case, usually, we would have a couple of officers come in and-"

"Yes it's only me. The other officers don't agree with my search plan, so…"

"You're on your own," Iris finished, a sympathetic smile reaching her eyes.

Rosalia sighed and smiled, but the smile didn't reach her eyes, "Yes, also, how long till I get the reports about the sample?"

"I'll try my best to send it in as soon as possible, Rosalia" Iris smiled as she stood up, "Thank you" Rosalia mumbled as she quietly left the room. Iris watched her walk out of the room, "She's scared", she mumbled to herself as she spun around in her chair. She grabbed the sample, her red nails digging into the plastic bag as she left for the lab. She scanned her ID at the lab entrance and pushed open the heavy door. The bright fluorescent lights hit her eyes, and she stepped in; the smell of decomposition hit her. The air was cool. Rows of stainless-steel counters gleaned under bright lights. Iris sat on a chair and pulled herself to the table as she looked down at the sample, her glasses slipping down her nose. She placed it aside as she pulled on her latex gloves, she slipped open the bag carefully, taking the fabric out, she squinted her eyes. "It's gauze…" she muttered, turning the fabric around. It was a small piece, dark and stained, the blood was congealed in patches, its color not red anymore. Iris examined it, as she put it on a steel dish, she turned to her computer and connected it to her digital microscope, she grabbed the cloth and aligned the sample under her lens. With the software running, she leaned back as the computer loaded the magnified image.

6:00 pm

William pulled out his phone, he sent a message to all the officers- *'We will continue this search tomorrow, at 7 am.'*

He had been searching the forest for a while. He didn't find a single clue or trace of where Sara was. He felt his forehead heat up as he drove to his cabin. He saw the sun go down through the trees as the mist around him thickened. He parked his car in front of his cabin and got down. He jogged up to the door and unlocked it and went in. Peace. Finally, after a whole day of searching. Well, it wasn't like he found anything, but he was sure he would find Sara. She might have escaped, but she won't survive in the woods for long. He walked back to the small kitchen, it was dimly lit, the orange-yellow light from the living room barely lighting it up, he took his mask off and threw it on the counter as he washed his hands. He looked out the window above the sink as he dried off his hands with a torn cloth. "No rain today…" he muttered staring up at the orange sky.

10:35 pm

Rosalia was sitting in her car; she had drifted off into sleep, her car was parked in the parking lot of Pine View Motel. The windows were down a little, and she felt a gentle and cool breeze brush against her face. She shifted uncomfortably in her seat when her phone vibrated. Her eyes widened as she grabbed her phone from her pocket. It wasn't Iris. It was her son texting her goodnight. Rosalia smiled, and texted him back, she put the phone aside and stared out the glass. She saw the mist thicken in front of her. She rubbed her palms together as she dug them into her pocket. "Damn, it's cold", she whispered as she turned on the car heat and rolled the windows back up. She watched her watch. Time was running out. She looked over to the side. "Oh my god," she jumped back as a lady stared at her from the side window. Rosalia's heart thumped loudly in her chest. It was the lady at the front desk in the motel. Rosalia opened her car door and got out. The lady stood to the side, her huge cheetah print purse thrown over her shoulder, "Why are you still out here?" she asked, Rosalia saw her stick the gum in her mouth to the back of her throat. "I'm a police officer, I need to stay on the lookout" she huffed. "Mhm, you know, parking your car in the motel's parking lot is gonna cost you," the lady said, eyeing her up and down. "What? You do realize that I'm a police officer and there's a missing person in the woods in front of your stupid Motel?" Rosalia pointed at the trees, her finger shivering. The lady sighed and spat her gum out. "Just saying. Pay up tomorrow morning." Rosalia rolled her eyes as she got back in her car.

People.

Rosalia never wanted all this to happen. *Why did Sara run into the woods? What did she see? Who was the stalker? Why was she not leading the case anymore? Why was everything spiralling out of control?*

12 am

William had fallen asleep. He felt a cool breeze enter his room from the windows, the trees were rustling, the owls hooting, the leaves crunching-

Wait. William got up, he heard leaves crunch outside, he squinted his eyes as he rolled over and grabbed a torch light, he rubbed the sleep out of his eyes and walked to the window next to his bed, he stared out, his eyes wandering in the darkness. It fell upon someone; his heart skipped a beat. "Oh my god", he whispered.

Sara.

Sara, it was Sara, she looked half dead, as she walked around, it was like she just woke up. William gasped, he ran downstairs and outside. He found her. "Anyone here?" he asked, trying to sound calm, so Sara wouldn't recognize his voice. Sara turned around, her breath heavy, her dark hair fell on her eyes. "Yes" she mumbled weakly.

12:15 am

Sara saw a man, she was saved. He had light green eyes and brown hair. He looked kind; he looked like a father. She walked to him, her foot dragging behind her. "I-I need help", she whispered, leaning on a tree. The man stared at her, it was like he was *happy.* Maybe he was just alone all the time, so he never really met anyone. He cleared his throat, "What happened?" he asked. "I, I'm lost, I ran away from some psycho kidnapper, stalker, I don't know, just, can you call the police, its urgent."

William sighed, she didn't recognise him, thank god. "Yes, of course, oh dear, come in…" Sara smiled weakly, *I'm saved.* She walked into the man's house. "Here sit down, I'll get you some water" he said, pointing at the couch. Sara nodded and sat down, she looked at the picture on the wall she had seen from outside. The family. She saw a man with his wife and son; she wondered who they were. The photo looked old, almost. She leaned forward and saw him in the kitchen pouring her a glass of water. "Who are they?" she asked, pointing at the picture. William's face shifted, it was like a grey cloud came over him as she gave her a glass of water, he didn't reply, his eyes shifted to the picture, he looked away and mumbled something. Sara gulped down the water. "Thank you, have you called the police yet-" she murmured, she felt her eyes get heavy, everything around her blurred, her ears were ringing. She heard the man say something but she couldn't figure out what, it all felt muffled, she looked up at the man, his green eyes. Oh my god.

His green eyes were the same green eyes she saw.

"You're the stalker-" she tried to say, she felt her eyes close, her head spinning. William nodded, smirking, but she couldn't see him, it was all a blur. She gripped onto the sofa, as she felt her head tumble back, she saw the orange light in the living room flash before her eyes as she fell asleep.

2am

Rosalia's eyes shot open as her phone rang. "Oh my god",- she muttered, sitting up in her car, as she put her hand to her chest, and she grabbed her phone. "Hello?" she said slowly, her eyes squinting at the bright phone light. "Is this officer Rosalia?"

"Iris?"

"Yes, I'm sorry I couldn't call you earlier, its late, but i figured you would be awake."

Rosalia sighed, "It's fine, have you-"

"Yes, yes, I have sent you the reports-"

Rosalia nodded, "I'll check them-"

"You have any questions, call me"

"Ok, thank you" Rosalia cut the call and saw the notification for the report. She sat up straight and looked away from her phone. *Please be helpful*. She exhaled and clicked on the report.

The Hastings Institute of Medicine and Forensic Science (HIMFS)

Forensic Report

Case number: 2090-ILM-126

Prepared by: Doctor Iris Chane, Forensic pathologist

Department: Forensic Science Unit

Location: Forensic lab 4A, 2nd building

Sample description: Blood sample found on gauze

Related case: Missing persons case

Suspected individual: Male, approximately ages 30-40

Analysed Sample Information

Blood type: AB-(AB negative)

Physical state: Blood on gauze showing signs of degradation and brown discolouration

Estimated time frame of blood age: Approximately 7 days to 9 days

Evidence Analysis

Colouration and degradation: The blood sample exhibited a brownish tint, indicating an advanced stage of hemolysis.

Observation: Blood started browning as early as 7 days post-deposition. Based on physical state and colouration, the sample is consistent with blood that has been exposed to environmental factors for about one week and 2 days.

Demographic Implications: Given that the blood type is AB-(AB negative); one of the rare blood types (approximately 4-7 per cent of the population) could be a pivotal piece of information.

End of report

Iris Chane

Forensic pathologist

Contact 41-01-90 for any queries

Rosalia clutched her phone tightly, her mind racing. She read the whole report again, her eyes glued to her phone. *AB negative.* That was the stalker's blood type. Male, ages 30-40. She called Iris. “Hello?” Iris asked, her voice echoing through Rosalia's car, “Yes, it’s me, I went through the report-”

“Right, any questions?”

“I was just wondering, can you send the reports to the police station, so they can check for *any* old convicts who match the description?”

“You’re a police officer, you can do it-”

“I’m not exactly a part of this case anymore”

“Right, you told me, I’ll see what I can do”

“Thank you”

Rosalia opened up the report again, her eyes scanning them as she read it *again.*

Chapter – 9

4:44 am

Sara's eyes shot open, but all she could see was darkness. Her eyelids fluttered weakly, struggling to adjust to the darkness. She scrambled around, her palms rubbing against the prickly wood floors. She tried to stand up, but her limbs felt heavy and unresponsive. A strange prickling sensation crawled across her skin, like tiny needles were stabbing her all over, making her skin feel raw and itchy. Her finger scratched against her legs. "Help", she tried to scream. Her voice was weak, and she felt her throat get scratchy. She broke out into a sweat across her forehead and neck, soaking her skin in cold, clammy streams. She tried to find something, her palms scrambled across the floor, she got on her knees and crawled, sweat dripping down her forehead onto the floor, she felt her head hit something, she felt around, it was a wall, she leaned back on it, her head hanging forward. She felt weak. She tried to take a deep breath, but it was like her throat was closed up. She felt tears well up in her eyes. Her breathing grew ragged as the panic set in. "no, this can't be happening."

She felt helpless, how many hours was she in here, how many days had passed? She should have known that the man was the one who was hunting her down, to, I don't know, possibly kill her. She slapped her palms over her forehead. "How could you be so stupid-" she mumbled to herself. She felt her tears pass the cuts on her face. She tried not to cry, her hands fumbling around to find something. Sara's body trembled as she tried to stand up, her knees buckled like a twig under her, forcing her forward. She fell head first onto the floor, her head slammed into the rough surface, as pain shot through her. Her vision blurred, her ears were ringing, and she felt blood trickle from her nose. She forced herself to get up again, her knees wobbling; she leaned on the wall, her shaky hands stretched out forward in the darkness as she tried to find *something.*

Sara walked around the borders of the room, leaning against the wall. It was small, musty and smelled like mould. Her hands reaching out, she couldn't find the door. She knelt, her fingers brushed against something, a box, or something, her hands felt around it, it was a stack of papers, she couldn't tell. She brought her face closer to the papers; she couldn't see them, obviously, since the darkness enveloped around her, she tried to see if there was anything else. Nothing. Not like she could do anything with these papers. Her lungs heaved with ragged breaths; she laid down, placing her head on the stack of papers. Her eyes closing slowly, she lost all hope.

6 am

Rosalia knew there was no point in going back into the woods, but she had to. She knew Sara was in there. She tugged her jacket closer as a cool breeze blew past her. She clutched her bag as she walked deeper into the woods. She had to look for more clues. *Anything* would help. Rosalia was deep in thought when an idea struck her mind. “Oh my god, that’s it, a search dog”, she turned back and started running to her car.

Rosalia swung open the door and stepped in. The other officers turned around and stared at her. She looked down at her outfit. She wasn't in uniform, and her collared white shirt was now brown at the collar, and her jeans were muddy at the hem. She didn't exactly have time to clean up, she slept in her car, and spent all day looking for Sara, her uniform was crumpled and tossed at the back of the car, it reeked of sweat. This outfit was the only other option she had. She looked up and smiled awkwardly. “Excuse me?” she said, walking to the nearest officer. The officer looked up from his desk. “Yes?”

“I’m Officer Rosalia. I was the lead on the.”

“Sara’s case, right?” he interrupted, looking back down at his computer

“Yes, I had an idea, I know it’s too soon, but-”

“Talk to Burt”

“What?” Rosalia squinted her eyes. She leaned away from the desk

“Talk to Officer William Burt, he’s the lead”

“Ok…where is he?” Rosalia asked, annoyed

“He hasn't come in yet; he should be here”

Rosalia scoffed; the head of the case was coming in late. She cleared her throat and sat down on a sofa. She stared out the windows of the police station as the morning fog cleared up. She leaned forward, her hands cupping her head, and she watched the clock as she waited for him.

6:56 am

A psychopath. They walk among us, perfectly normal, yet their minds are a labyrinth of dark secrets and lies, never revealing the monster within.

William made sure she couldn't escape. He locked the small door when he put Sara in the basement of his cabin. There were no lights, she couldn't tell the time, or anything. She was stuck there until-

William reached the station. He was late, but he was there. He brushed his finger through his hair and stepped out of his car as he walked in. “Hey officers, good morning”, he smiled as the other officers smiled and waved. He saw Rosalia on the couch, her head hung forward. He looked around. “She wanted to speak to you, apparently, she has an ‘*idea*’ or something”, the officer at the desk said in a whisper. William nodded and walked to her. “Officer Rosalia?” he called out. No response. She was sleeping. William shook his head, trying to hide his smirk, and he clapped his hands near her ear. Rosalia's eyes fluttered open as she stood up. “William”, She said, trying to hide the fact that she fell asleep. William pursed his lips, “Good morning”, he wished her sarcastically.

Rosalia rolled her eyes. “I fell asleep waiting for you. You're not very punctual, are you?”

William smiled, “I was busy, had to take care of something important, anyways… heard you had to talk to me, about something, an idea?”

“Yes, about Sara, I know-”

Williams’ hand shot up in the air, and he asked her to wait. “Why don't you wait in my office? We’ll talk there, it is the last office to the left, I’ll be there in a couple of minutes.”

Rosalia sighed and walked to his office. She pushed the door and sat down in front of his desk, her eyes wandered around the office as she moved around in the uncomfortable wooden chair. “This man really knows how to waste time” she muttered looking down at her watch, she saw a pinboard on his wall, a bunch of newspaper clippings were pinned, she got up and walked towards it. They were cases, and other things, her eyes wandered around them as she read them. She had time to kill; she knew William wasn't going to come any time soon, even though he said ‘a couple of minutes.’

Her eyes scanned down to a newspaper clipping that didn't look very new. It was yellow and torn, Rosalia tilted her head as she looked at it.

Highway Tragedy: Two Family Members Killed and One Missing After September 21 Incidents

She read the headline. Why did William have this? And why did it sound familiar? She looked on top of the newspaper and saw the date. 2005, September 21.

2005.

20 years ago.

Her eyes widened. This was-

She pulled out the newspaper clipping, it was half torn, but she knew it was the case. Sara's. It was the.....

Rosalia couldn't think; her mind was foggy. Why did William have this clipping from 2005, unless he worked on it? How old was William? He can't be that old. He looked at least thirty or thirty five, this case happened twenty years ago, he would have been a teenager, so why would he have worked on it? Or had some connection to it. Was it just a coincidence that this was all connected to Sara? Rosalia heard footsteps outside. She stuffed the clipping into her pocket and sat down. William swung open the door. "Sorry about the wait, I had to speak to the officers about today's search plan. Anyway, what was it that you wanted to talk about?" He sat down in front of her. Rosalia straightened her back, her palms were sweaty, she looked up at him, "It's about Sara, I have a plan on how we can try to locate her quicker."

"I'm listening," William said, leaning back in his chair.

"We could use search and rescue dogs, it's efficient and"

William laughed.

"I don't get it...what is so funny?"

"Really, officer? This isn't the big city, you know, it isn't London, we barely have enough police officers, you think we have trained search and rescue dogs here?"

Rosalia was taken aback, “We-”

“No, officer Rosalia, *we* can’t do anything. Anyways, I’m sure Sara is safe, you're a little emotional about this, don't you think?”

Rosalia scoffed, “Seriously?”

William shrugged, “I mean, Sara is your friend, you care too much, you should leave this case to us, we are handling it.”

“Handling it? You have made no progress; it's like you don't even care that she went missing.”

“The last time I checked, you are not in charge of this case, neither do you work for us, you came here all the way from the city. This is our town, our station, and we will take care of this”

“Fine, I also have something else, I went to the woods, I found gauze, it had blood on it, I sent it to the forensic lab, and they got it tested. Could you check if the reports match any old convicts?”

William nodded slowly, “Do you have the reports?”

“Yes, I got a copy” she pulled out a printed piece of paper and slid it across the desk to him, William grabbed it, “I’ll check and let you know.”

Rosalia stood up, the wooden chair screeching against the tiles, she sighed and stepped out the door. She left the police station and sat in her car and pulled out the crumpled up newspaper clipping from her pocket. “I wonder why you had this *officer,* William.”

Chapter – 10

A rare blood type, hiding cursed secrets.

William clutched the report. “Oh no.” It was a small town. Not many people had the blood type, AB negative, it was one of the rarer types, well, not everyone except him. He brushed his palms over his forehead. He had to be careful. The gauze was his. He had cut his arm, and it wouldn't stop bleeding. He wrapped it with gauze; it must have gotten stuck on the tree when-

But there isn't any proof that the gauze is connected to Sara being missing, he smirked. If anyone found out it was his blood, he could say he went into the woods cause he lived there, everyone would believe him over Rosalia. No one would even suspect him.

8:24 am

Sara woke up, her head pounding in pain, and she felt her forehead heat up. She turned around and sat up It was still dark. She leaned on the wall behind her, and she rested her arm on the stack of papers beside her. She didn't know how much time had passed, her ears were numb, the room was silent, she held her arms close to her, when her fingers brushed against her watch.” My-my watch, it has a light-” she whispered her finger trying to find the button on the digital watch, her finger brushed against the side of the watch, a blinking blue light flashed and stopped in five seconds, it wasn't bright, but, she could use it, when she pressed the button again and the light turned on, she saw the time. 8:30 am. She slowly stood up and pressed the button again, the light shone as she pointed it at the walls. They were a dark shade of grey, she kept pressing the light every five seconds as she pointed it at the walls trying to find a door, or an exit. Nothing. It was like this room did not have a door. She sat down next to the stack of papers, defeated, her eyes were welled up with tears, she felt dead. She didn't know what to do. She pressed the button again, the faint blue light lighting up in front of her. She moved her wrist to the papers, the light turned off, she pressed the button again. The papers were newspapers, old ones, she turned towards them and shone the light again, her hands grazing against the newspapers, she saw the headlines, her heart stopped.

Highway Tragedy

She saw the first two words, she pressed the button on her watch and shined the light on the paper again and read the next words.

Two Family Members Killed and One Missing

The light turned off again, she pressed the button and shone it on the last letters.

After the September 21 Incident

She knew those words all too well. She had read this clipping more than a hundred times twenty years ago. It was engraved in her brain. She fell back, trying to process what was happening. She leaned forward back to the stack of newspapers and took another one out from the bottom.

She pressed the button on her watch and shone the light on the paper.

Road accident turns tragic: Two confirmed dead, one missing, September 21

Sara took another paper out of the stack

Highway crash claims the lives of two Indian doctors: Investigation is active

Sara's eyes were filled with tears, she wiped them away and took another newspaper from the pile

Police Probe after 2 Killed, 1 Missing

She clasped her hand against her mouth as she leaned back. They were all clippings from *that* incident. 20 years ago. September 21, 2005. Sara closed her eyes.

I was just ten. Sanya was right beside me, we went out to celebrate mumma's birthday. She was sitting in front next to dadwhile he was driving. We were going to get dessert at the ice cream shop I loved. I was leaning on the front seat and looking at Sanya. She was telling me something about her ice cream obsession. Mumma was saying we should not eat ice cream now, since it's chilly out, dad disagreed, "I'll eat ice cream even if I'm in Antarctica," he laughed. Mumma shook her head in disapproval. Sanya and I broke out in laughter. I saw bright headlights head towards us, I heard a loud crash, Sanya held my hand, I heard mumma shout, dad screamed, Sanya looked at me and said something, I couldn't hear her, I heard ringing, I saw the glass break and pierce through my arm, I saw dads head swing back as the airbags opened up, I heard honking, crashing, glass breaking, mumma screaming, dad cursing. Then, I didn't hear anything. I felt Sanya's hand leave mine.

Sara opened her eyes. She was in tears. She put all the papers back together. The person who took her, they must know something, maybe they were someone her parents knew, or something, Sara couldn't think, her mind was blank, she crouched down onto the floor, her hands trembling, *where was she?*

9 am

A cold breeze whispers cries that vanish before you can hear them.

Rosalia found herself driving back to the woods, she parked her car on the empty road and got out, she stuffed her hands into her pockets as she felt a breeze rustle through the trees, she slammed the car door shut and walked into the woods. It was 9 am, but the woods were still dark, it was like once she stepped into them, the sun disappeared through the tall, thick trees. Rosalia grabbed her phone and switched on the torchlight as she walked deeper in, remembering the way she came in.

Sara felt destroyed, she was lying on the floor in a puddle of her own tears, she had given up. She tried everything. Her legs were numb, and her eyes were swollen. Even if her eyes were open, it was the same, darkness. She knew she had to wait in here until the stalker came back. *Would he even come back?* Sara tried not to think about that. When she heard something, not from inside the room, someone outside, a muffled sound, Sara's ears perked up. She slowly sat up, leaning back on the wall. She didn't hear anything; she closed her eyes and sighed. She heard it again. It was from the other side of the room, Sara got on her knees and crawled to the other side, her knees scraping against the woods, she placed her palms on the wall and pressed her ear against the wall. Someone was on the other side. "It might be him" Sara whispered, she threw herself against the wall screaming "LET ME OUT" she shouted, her voice raspy, she hit her fists against the wall, she screamed and screamed and screamed, till she lost her voice, she sat back down, she heard the sound again, she leaned closer to the wall, someone was out there. She knew it. She heard a door unlock from the other side of the wall, she heard it creak, and then she heard it slam shut. Maybe the stalker left. "That psycho must have left", she muttered, trying to catch her breath as she lay back down on the floor.

9:45 am

Rosalia felt her phone vibrate, she was getting a call. "How is there a signal in here?" She whispered, looking at her phone. *Iris.*

Iris was calling her. "Hello? Iris?"

"Yes, it's me, I need you to come to my lab, now"

"I'm busy now, is it something-?"

"Rosalia, you need to come now"

"Iris, I'm in Crimson Woods, searching for any clues about Sara. I can't take a U-turn and come back now."

"It's about the blood sample. I was somehow able to run it through the system. It's not a match to any of the present or old convicts in Hastings or Juniper Ridge, I double checked, we don't have a lot of AB negatives here, but…we do have a match"

"What? Who is it?"

"Officer William Burt, under the Hastings police department"

Rosalia's eyes widened, "What? Him?" her voice dropped

"Yes, it is pretty weird to find a police officer's blood-stained gauze in the middle of the woods, but do you know him?"

"Yes, yes, he's the obnoxious officer who took over the case, and-"

Rosalia fished out the newspaper clipping from her pocket with trembling hands and stared at it, her thumb brushing over the folded crease covering the date.

"And?" Iris asked.

"I think he's connected to Sara's disappearance"

William knew it wasn't a good idea to leave Sara alone. He knew she couldn't escape, but he had to go anyway, to give her food, so she wouldn't die. He grabbed his car keys and stepped out of the station. He saw another officer outside, and he waved. "Hey Officer William, where are you headed?"

"To search for Sara, I sent the rest of the officers out to look at the south side, we might get some leads down there" William replied with a straight face.

Chapter – 11

Seven minutes. They say seven minutes after death, the brain can still show signs of activity. Tiny signals that remind us life isn't gone, yet.

11:00 am

Sara laid still on the floor, her head was throbbing, she curled up, holding her knees close, she felt her mouth go dry. Sara heard someone outside. She sat up and crawled to the wall. She put her ear up against it.

11:10 am

William walked into his silent cabin and locked the door, he went into the kitchen and grabbed a half empty bottle of water and tucked it under his arm, he grabbed a few slices of stale bread and put it on a plate, he walked to the back of his cabin, and set the plate and bottle down, he grabbed a bunch of keys from his pocket and fumbled with them till he found the right key, he clicked open the first door, and grabbed the plate and bottle and stepped in, he walked down the dark staircases as the flashlight on his phone lit up the tight space, he reached out for the doorknob and unlocked it, he put his phone flashlight inside the room and saw Sara in the corner of the room, her head was down. He smirked.

Sara blinked open her eyes as she heard someone. She looked up and flinched. She saw a flashlight at the entrance of the door. *So that's where the door is.* She tried to stand up, but she couldn't; she weakly crawled to the door. The man bent down and slid her a water bottle and a plate. He shut the door, the darkness enveloped her again, and she heard him lock it. “No, no, open the door, please”, Sara begged as she crawled closer to the door. She banged her fists against the door, “Please, please, open the door”, she cried, her voice weak. She fell backwards and sighed. She couldn't even see where he had slid her the food. She rummaged around the room, her hands reaching out, she felt her hands wrap around a bottle of water, she grabbed it quickly and her dry lips gulped it down. She crawled around, her hands stretched out as she tried to find the plate, she found it, and felt around, two slices of bread. The bread was stale, but she ate in silence, accepting her fate.

Rosalia went to the police station. Her head was pounding, she walked in and past the front desk, and she heard the police officer ask her what she wanted. She went to Williams' office and slammed his door open “William, I-” she stopped, he wasn't there. She turned around and saw another officer staring at her. “Where is he?” she asked the officer. “He went for the search with the other officers”, he replied. “Where did they go?”

“South, I think”

“South? Sara disappeared in the woods, she’s not in the town”

The officer shrugged, “Officer William knows what he is doing, and aren't you the officer who got kicked out of the search?”

Rosalia looked around. “Do you know where he lives?”

“What?”

“You heard me, where does he live?”

“I’m not telling you that, in fact, I don't know exactly either”

“Ok…don't tell me, it's fine, but can you at least help me with something?”

“What?”

Rosalia starts walking, the officer follows, she walks to her car and stops.

The officer looks around in confusion, “What do you want me to do?”

“Tell me where he lives, now.”

“I can't do that.”

Rosalia sees his hands reach down for his gun, she smirks, she leans forward and grabs it, pointing it at him, “Get in the car.”

The officer steps back.

“Move back one more time, I’ll shoot you, get in the car”

He gets in the car, Rosalia gets in the front seat and starts driving. “Now, tell me where he lives”

He looks at her, “I don’t know exactly, William never told anyone-”

“Tell me, now”

“Ok, ok, it is somewhere in Crimson Woods, I know that.”

“Crimson woods? He lives there?”

“Yes, he does”, the officer muttered. Rosalia turned to him, “What is your name?”

“Ben, why do you want to go to William's house now?” he asked. Rosalia heard the fear in his voice. She sighed, “He’s connected to Sara’s disappearance.”

Ben laughed, but he stopped quickly when he remembered Rosalia had a gun. “No, he’s not.”

“Well, let's find out, shall we?”

Part-2

Sanya Singh, 2005

I don't remember much anymore. I was fifteen, all of us were in the car, I was talking to Sara, telling her something. We were laughing, and that's when I saw headlights. Bright yellow headlights, they lit up the whole car, blinding us, I looked at Sara, her little pretty eyes closed shut, "I love you Sara, it's gonna be okay," I remember saying as I held her hand tightly, I saw her little arm get pierced with a shard of glass, I heard so much glass break, I felt my leg twist and sprain, it might have been broken. The door on my side flung open, I saw the forest on the side of the road. Funny, I didn't even know which forest it was. I felt my head throb in pain, I knew my parents wouldn't survive, I saw blood seeping out of mumma's mouth, and I couldn't even see dads face, I saw glass, and his arm hanging on the side. Sara was unconscious. And that's when I ran. I don't know why, I ran, I ran out of the car after it collided with the lorry. If only I hadn't let go of Sara's hand.

I remember running; I never looked back. I still remember the last time I saw little Sara's face in the car, her eyes were shut tightly, and she had blood on her arm. I ran through the woods. It was dark, and I heard the sounds of the accident soften out as I ran deeper and deeper. My memories also faded, for a second I stopped running, I couldn't remember anything, who I was, where I was, nothing, I didn't stop running, it was like my legs wouldn't stop, I think I ran for more than thirty minutes, I stopped running when I slip and fell near a stream, my head hit a wet rock and everything went black.

I woke up in bed. I was tucked in a red, thick blanket. The ceiling above me looked old, the walls in the room were made of wood, like a cabin of sorts, there was a dim light hung opposite to the bed. I couldn't remember anything. I felt stupid, helpless, I wanted to know who I was, I sat up and looked around, I got out of the bed and stumbled to the door, I slowly opened it, I was now in a hallway, I saw a beautiful woman, not older than twenty five, she was in the kitchen, her face was red, she had long brown hair, a boy was hiding behind her, he looked my age, they didn't notice me, I saw a vase fly past me and hit the woman, I stumbled back, the vase broke into a million pieces as it hit the woman's head, she fell down and the little boy got on his knees and held her, "wake up mom" he cried, I looked at the other end of the room, there was a man, he looked angry, his eyes were red, he grabbed a photo frame and threw it across as it hit the little boy, the boy fell back as the corner of the frame hit his forehead, he cried in pain, "what are you doing?" I screamed as I ran towards the boy and the woman on the floor. The man looked livid. I turned to the woman, she had a faint smile on her face, as she whispered, "I found you fallen at the stream as I was gathering firewood, you looked hurt, I brought you in, dear-"

The man screamed, he grabbed the umbrella on the side and threw it at her, as he stormed out of the house. I stared at the door as he left. "He gets a little…angry," the woman whispered, still smiling. "Little?" I mumbled as I helped her sit up, "Why was he so angry?" I asked, as I watched the woman help the little boy up, "I...he was angry that I brought you in without telling him," she whispered. I held onto her hand as she spoke.

The woman simply nodded. "Mom, I'm going to my room", the little boy whispered as he left. The woman turned to me, "Are you a trekker, perhaps a camper, dear?"

"What?"

"Why were you in the woods that late at night?"

"I....I don't know."

"You don't know?"

"I don't remember anything."

"Not even your name?"

I tried to think, I closed my eyes tight, "No."

The man came back again in the evening. He walked past me and grabbed the woman by her neck. "You forgot"

"What - what did I forget?" She tried to speak.

The man rolled his eyes. I watched his grip tighten around her neck, I ran to him, "let go, let go," I shouted as I tried to pull his hand away, he simply kicked my knees, and I fell back. I saw the woman's eyes close as her neck swung back; she was dead. The man let go, his eyes widened, he stepped back, he kicked the woman, "wake up, you idiot" he shouted, I watched him for the next thirty minutes as he tried to wake her up, "she's dead" I mumbled, tears in my eyes, the man turned to me, "what did you say?"

"You killed her, you psychopath."

The man charged towards me, choking me as he pinned me against the wall, "What did you say, you little-"

"DAD."

It was the boy, he was on the stairs, the man let go of my neck when he saw his son. The boy came running down as he saw his mom lying dead on the floor, "WHAT DID YOU DO TO HER?" the boy asked, crying. The man crouched down next to him and put his arm around his son, "I'm sorry, your mother is dead, William."

William was his name.

William was crying as he held his mother's limp body in his pale hands, his knuckles red, his dad stood above him, his face covered with his palms, he kept on saying sorry, over and over again. I stared at the scene in horror. My eyes kept shifting from William's crying face to his dead mothers. I crouched down on the floor and cried. It had been more than an hour, and I was still on the floor, staring at the tiles, and William had gone upstairs. The man dragged the woman's body outside as he dug up a hole in the back of the cabin. I looked out the door frame as he threw the woman's body into the hole and filled it back up. He looked at me, "This never happened," he said as he walked past me, into the house. I turned back and followed him, "You killed her," I screamed, pointing my finger at him. I was shaking in fear.

"No, I did not. She died because she was sick."

"What? I saw you choke her, stop lying-"

"You'll keep your mouth shut, or I will bury you next to that woman."

I watched him leave the cabin as he locked the door from outside. I went upstairs and saw William sitting on a small chair as he stared out the window. "How old are you?" I asked, "Fifteen", he replied, facing me, "And you?"

"Same."

"What's your name?"

"I...I don't remember, I think I lost my memory-"

"Really?"

I nodded, looking out the window, staring at the trees and the sky. We stayed silent for a while.

"It's Sanya..."

"What is?"

"My name it's Sanya."

"Sanya", he repeated, nodding slowly.

"Do you have a map? I need to get out of here, I don't know my way around the woods."

"What, I mean, yes, I do think I have a map, but where will you go? You don't even remember what happened to you."

"I...I think I need to go to the police."

William stood up, his hand gripping onto the chair, his knuckles red, his eyes narrowing, "Why?"

"Your dad, he killed your mom-"

"You're going to go to the police about that?" he asked. I saw something change in his face; he didn't look so kind anymore.

"Ye-yes."

"No, you're not," he walked closer

"What? I have to-"

"I said no."

"William, your dad killed-"

"He's all I have left," he said, his teeth clenching, a lone tear rolling down his cheek.

"William-"

Then he swung a baseball bat over my head. Threw me into a dark room, locked me in there for the next twenty years. I was never really gone. I was right there.

Half alive, half dead, half gone.

Open the door.

Open the door.

Open the door.

Open the door.

Please.

Please.

Please.

William.

William.

I won't go to the police, I swear.

That's all that came out of my mouth for a month.

I was allowed to come outside once a week, to clean up, at gunpoint, so even if I tried running, I'd be shot dead. The memories slowly came back, and I remembered everything once I hit the twenty - day mark in the room. William and his dad would take turns throwing food into the room, then his dad got really sick and died. I was a prisoner.

Until I escaped. 20 years later, that is.

I don't know how it happened, but when William opened the door to throw in my lunch, I lunged at him. Of course, I had tried this before, but he had a gun; this time, he didn't, he looked exhausted almost this time. I lunged at him and grabbed the ceramic plate he brought and bashed it into his skull, I kicked him again and again and ran, I ran and ran and ran. Just like how I had run twenty years ago, away from the car crash, away from Sara. I kicked open the door and ran. William stumbled as he tried to come after me. I grabbed a knife from the kitchen and held it pointing at William, his eyes were red, and puffy, "Don't come closer" I shouted, he raised his arms up, "Sanya, get back in"

"No"

"Sanya, you won't survive out there. Come back"

"I'll tell everyone about what you did, about what your dad did."

"Sanya, get back in. Now"

I threw the knife at him, and it pierced his arm. He fell to the floor, crying in pain. I stared at him, and stopped back, grabbing another knife. I started to run for the main door, "I know where your sister is, Sanya."

I turned around, "What!"

"If you try anything, even go to the police, trust me, Sara will be dead. I'll make sure I find her. If you step out of the door, I'll find her, I will."

I scoffed at his face and ran out of the house into the woods, and the cool breeze hit my face. I ran deeper into the woods and sat down. I decided not to go to the police yet. I had to follow William and see what he would do. She stared at her hands "Where are you, Sara?"

12:42 pm

Sanya hadn't left the woods. She could have found her way out of them and gone to the police or…to someone. But she didn't. She knew if William found out, he would hurt Sara; he knew where Sara was. He knew it all, he…he would keep Sara locked up if it was to shut Sanya up and not get her to say a word to the police.

She would wander around, sleep on the cold forest ground, take shelter from rain, and try not to starve. She didn't know how, but she had to find Sara before William did.

But she didn't know, he already had locked her up in the same place she was.

Chapter – 12

2:00 pm

Rosalia clutched the gun tightly in her sweaty hands as she followed Ben.

"I really don't know where he lives, exactly," Ben muttered

"I don't need an exact location, just…just go, give me an approximate location or something," Rosalia said, nodding her head towards the path he was walking in.

"Why do-"

"No questions, just walk, and find me his cabin"

"I seriously don't think he-"

"I said go"

2:35 pm

Sanya was walking, her hair was in a loose braid, her red shirt was moist, and her jeans were torn. She looked up in the sky, grey clouds were hiding the sun, and it was getting darker. She felt raindrops fall on her head, and then she heard something that wasn't just raindrops falling.

Footsteps.

She wouldn't let anyone see her, not until she made sure Sara was *safe*, and Willaim would do anything to her. She hid behind a tree, her breathing turned shallow.

She saw two people, a man walking in front, and a woman. She watched them walk past her as she clutched onto the tree trunk she was behind. Sanya sighed slowly as she watched them walk past her. She stepped out from behind the tree and started to follow them, trying to mask the sound of her footsteps. The rain started to pour down on the forest, grey clouds completely covering the sky, and the wind howled.

Sanya felt herself tumble over and trip, her face hitting the moist forest floor. She quickly rolled over to the side before the woman in front of her could catch a glimpse of her.

2:40 pm

Rosalia turned around. She heard something, she pulled out her gun from her pocket and held it up in the air. Ben looked at her, "What?"

"I heard something," she gripped her gun tighter, her knuckles whitening, her voice barely more than a whisper.

"It's raining, maybe a branch fell or something," he mumbled as his eyes flickered around nervously. Rosalia walked slowly towards the sound, her breath slowing down, her eyes darting around the shadowed woods, and raindrops pattered in the background. She caught a glimpse of a figure hiding, and she pointed her gun at the person.

“Who are you?”Rosalia shouted, her hands trembling. The woman looked ragged, her hair was knotted and black, dark streaks of mud and dirt smudged on her olive skin, a lot of scars on her arms, and blood stains on her shirt. The woman stared at Rosalia with her vacant, dark eyes; her eyes widened, it was like she had never seen a human before.

2:47 pm

Sanya stared at the woman. It had been *years* since she had looked into another human's eyes. She couldn't stop looking. She caught a glimpse of the man behind the woman. He looked scared. He stood behind her, staring down at her. Sanya slowly stood up, her hands raised as the woman straightened her arm with the gun in it. Sanya slowly parted her lips, “I’m just lost,” she lied.

The woman lowered her gun. “Where were you headed?”

Sanya straightened her back and cleared her voice, “I was camping, and I can’t find my campsite anymore”

The woman sighed and put her gun away. She looked at the man.

2:55 pm

She was just a lost camper.

Not Sara.

Not dangerous.

Rosalia turned to Ben, “You know what, take her with you, and help her out, I’ll figure out where William lives,” she paused, “I know you're gonna report me to the police for bringing you with me, but…please, if you're gonna report me, do it after 6 pm. Please."

Ben swallowed hard, "Ok"

Rosalia turned to the woman, "He'll get you somewhere safe, he's a police officer, you can go with him"

3:00 pm

A police officer. Lost hope in them long ago.

Sanya nodded and followed the man. She watched the woman walk away. The man turned to her, "So, what's your name?"

"Um, Sam," she lied.

"Why did you go camping alone? You do know Crimson Woods isn't very safe, people usually come here for hunting and stuff."

"Yeah, I don't know, and…who is she?" Sanya asked, turning back as she watched the woman walk off into the distance.

"Oh, some psycho police officer from the city, Rosalia"

"Why is she here?"

"She's trying to solve a case…which she clearly doesn't know a thing about"

"You don't seem to like her"

"I don't"

"Where is she going?"

"To another officer's house, she thinks he's related to the case"

Sanya nodded, then she stopped. Who lives in the woods? She turned to the man, "Wait…his house is in the woods?"

"Yes, he lives in some cabin; no one really knows the exact location."

"He's a police officer?"

"Yes, a very good one"

"What's his name?"

"William"

Sanya felt time stop.

William?

William was a police officer?

"Why did…why did she…go looking for him?" Sanya whispered.

"She thinks he's related to the case…" the man said, his eyes were narrow, he was weirded out by all her questions.

"What case?"

"A missing person case…and I think we need to get going, it's raining a lot, and it's not going to stop-"

"Who is missing?" Sanya whispered, her eyes red, her fists curled up.

"Lady…I think we need to go, you're acting kind of-"

Sanya gripped the man's collar and shoved him against a tree, "Tell me"

Sanya's eyes scanned the man's eyes, her grip tightening around his collar, the blood from her fingers seeping into the fabric.

"What, you crazy-"

"Who is missing?"

"Let go of me-"

"Tell me, who is missing?"

"Sara Singh"

Sanya felt her world shatter. She stepped back, her eyes disoriented, he…William….he…

She turned back to see if she could still see Rosalia walking, but she couldn't. She ran towards the direction of where she was walking. She heard the man calling behind her.

She felt the rain get heavier, and her vision blurred. She tried to run faster to catch up to Rosalia, her mind was racing, she saw her in the distance, walking in the rain, she shouted, "Wait-"

The woman turned around and saw her. Sanya ran closer and stopped, "I - I -"

"What?"

"You're looking for William," Sanya huffed, trying to catch her breath

"Yes, I am-"

"And for Sara"

Sanya saw something change in Rosalia's face when she said Sara, she saw her nod her head slowly, "How do you know…about…."

"I'm Sanya"

Not gone. Half gone.

Rosalia's eyes widened, she tried to say something, but she couldn't, she looked at Sanya, trying to register her face, "No, you can't be, Sanya, she-"

"I was never gone, they thought I was a runaway, didn't they?"

"Oh my god, you…you do look like her," Rosalia said, stepping closer.

Sanya smiled, her voice weak, "Sara looks like me."

Rosalia nodded slowly, staring deep into Sanya's eyes.

"I was never dead, or missing, or gone, I was right here."

"Where…what…"

"William"

"Oh my god, he–"

"He has Sara too, I know it, and if we don't get to him quick, he might…"

Rosalia nodded, "Do you know where his cabin is?"

"Yes."

Chapter – 13

Would she also disappear like Sanya, without a single trace? Just as the police never found her, no one saw her, no one cared. People would forget about her after a few months, her case would be thrown under the rug, it would just be another unsolved, not important, "runaway" named case. Maybe it was fate.

Sara felt dead; she fell in and out of consciousness. William hadn't given her food in a while, and she felt sick. She would try to scream for help, but it was useless; she had lost all hope. Hope in the police, in the people who might have seen her, in herself, in Rosalia. Where was she? Had she given up? Had she already forgotten?

Then Sara heard something, a lock opening, footsteps down stairs, another lock opening, and the door swung open, Sara saw William standing, the light behind him shining into the dark room, she saw him standing with bags, he said something, "get up," Sara slowly stood up, she watched him open the door completely, light hitting her face, "Come fast," he whispered, clutching a knife in his other hand, Sara walked slowly, her heart racing, was she being let go? No, probably not. No chance, none. Maybe she was going to be killed now? Maybe.

William grabbed her arm and threw her out of the room, and dragged her up the stairs. She couldn't open her eyes; she had been in the dark for too long, much too long. She watched him as he dragged her up the stairs, and through the cabin floors, then outside, she saw the clouds, and rain, the sun shining in the corner as it was covered by cloudy grey clouds, she heard thunder rumble, she felt herself be dragged through the muddy floor, then he stopped, he grabbed keys, and threw her into his car, Sara tried to do something, stand up, scream, something, but she couldn't. She felt herself being thrown into the trunk of the car, and she watched him as he shut the trunk door on her face. She was in the dark, again.

4:38 pm

They found the cabin, it was raining, and the cabin looked beautiful, with the orange sun rays falling on it.

They walked in, and the door was open.

But everything was…empty.

"He left," Sanya whispered, tears rolling down her cheek, "He must have taken Sara"

"What?" Rosalia walked in, and she saw everything was packed, all the drawers were open and empty, "Where… where did he…keep you?" she asked slowly, trying to keep her voice from trembling. Sanya walked past her and saw the kitchen. She turned right, and she saw the dark hallway. The same dark hallway. The hallway where she had seen the woman, and the boy hiding behind her, the vase flew past her and hit the woman, *twenty years ago*. Sanya followed the dark hallway all the way to the end. She heard Rosalia follow her. Sanya saw the first door; it swung open, and she saw the dark staircase leading down to the place she had spent *twenty years* in. She walked down the staircase and saw the door. The same door which kept her locked up. It was open, she walked forward and stepped into the room. Dark and musty. She turned back and faced Rosalia, "he kept her in here"

"Sara? He kept Sara in here?"

"Yes, if only we had come here earlier, we could have," Sanya felt her throat get tight, "we could have saved her"

"So…he…he kept you in here, too? All those years…"

Sanya simply nodded, still staring into the room. She could hear her heart pounding in her ears.

Rosalia pulled out her phone, turning on the flashlight as she pointed it into the room, "Where did he go with her?"

"I don't know," Sanya said, looking up, her eyes filled with tears.

They go back up and outside. Sanya stares at the empty spot where the car used to be. "He took her somewhere. He's scared I'll tell the police about him"

"But we need to tell the police about…"

"We can't, if William finds out, he *will* kill Sara"

The rain fell softly, as the two stood hopelessly, no words, no movements, just quiet in the rain, like the world had forgotten they were even there.

"She's going to be gone, just like I was," Sanya said, crying. Her voice echoed through the empty woods. Rosalia held her hand and squeezed it tightly, tears streaming down her face.

5 pm

Sara felt her eyes flicker open. She was tied to a chair, her ankles tightly bound, her wrists bleeding from the tight rope around them. She was alone in a small wooden room. It was the room William had first put her in. Wasn't it? Sara couldn't think, her mind was all over the place, she had a cloth tied around her mouth, she heard rain hit the roof of the room, her eyes darted around, she couldn't escape, even if she tried, she was too tired, too hurt, her legs were weak, her arms scraped up.

She had given up.

Had everyone already forgotten she had gone missing?

She tried. Again. To escape. But she could not.

5:30 pm

William drove back to the cabin, his hands were trembling as he tried to get a grip on the steering wheel. Bundles of rope were on the seat next to him, the wipers on his car swooshing, rain battering on his car. He had forgotten the most important thing. The lighter. He had three petrol cans in the seat behind him, and he had to drive fast. He kept Sanya silent for twenty years to hide the truth. The truth about his dad killing his mom. Sanya had seen it all. So, he kept her silent. He had to protect his father. But *deep* down, William felt like he was falling apart; the weight of those years was too much for him. He wanted to end it. First, Sara had to be *gone.*

6 pm

Ben stared at his watch as he stood outside the police station. He was shivering as the rain poured down on him. He had walked all the way back. It was exactly 6 pm. No William, no Rosalia, no weird lady who ran back to Rosalia in the woods.

Ben walked into the station, his hair dripping cold water. "Did Officer William stop by?" he asked the officer at the front desk. "No, he didn't stop by, why?"

"I need to report something," Ben said, swallowing hard.

"Go on?"

"Rosalia held me at gunpoint, took me to Crimson Woods, forced me to show her Officer Williams' house."

The officer stared at Ben, his mouth hanging open.

6:07 pm

Rosalia's hand never left Sanyas.

They stood under the cabin, both of them helpless. They didn't know a thing. Where Sara was, where William was…they knew nothing. Sanya saw something in between the trees, and rain, lights, orange headlights. Her eyes widened as she pointed to the light. Rosalais' eyes followed her hand and saw the orange lights. As they came closer, she grabbed Sanya's arm and ran behind the cabin, "What are you-"

"Shhh," Rosalia whispered, her voice trembling as she watched the lights come closer and closer. Then he stepped out. William. Rosalia watched closely through the thick rain to see if someone else, *Sara*, was there. "Is it him?" Sanya whispered, Rosalia nodded, and she watched him go inside the cabin. She turned around and faced Sanya. She grabbed both her hands and looked into her eyes, "Sanya, trust me with this," she whispered. Sanya looked confused, "What?"

"You need to go back"

"What?"

Rosalia looked back and saw William come back from inside the cabin. She turned to Sanya, she had seconds, and pushed her from the side, sending her stumbling forward, just in front of the cabin, opposite William. William turned around swiftly as he saw Sanya, fallen down at the side. He dropped his keys as he watched Sanya get up slowly. She opened up her mouth, but she didn't say anything; she let out a trembling breath. William let out a low, mocking whistle. "Well, look at that," he walked to her and grabbed Sanya's arm. Rosalia ran from the back side of the cabin and to the car so William would not see her. She opened up the trunk and slid in. Sanya watched her from the corner of her eyes as William faced her. He kicked Sanya, and she fell down. He kicked her again, and again and again.

She let him.

He picked her up and dragged her to the car, and threw her in the backseat as he grabbed a rope and tied up her arms and legs. He sat in the front seat and started driving, looking at Sanya from the rearview mirror. "You made a huge mistake, you know…I was only going to kill your sister, but now you showed up, so might as well…"

Sanya watched his eyes from the rear view mirror as they stared at her. She didn't say a word. She watched him drive through the thick rain.

Rosalia waited for the car to stop; she knew, or at least, she *hoped*, William was going to take Sanya to the same place where Sara was. She felt the car come to a stop.

Sanya saw William stop his car in the middle of nowhere, he stepped out and locked the car, grabbed the cans of petrol in the back seat and left her in it, she watched him walk to a small, worn-down a wooden shed, Sanya kicked the under of her seat so Rosalia could hear her from the trunk, Rosalia kicked back, she slowly opened up the trunk, her arms almost snapping as she pushed it open just enough so she could roll out, she fell and ducked down under the car.

Sanya saw William come out with an empty chair. He placed it a few feet away from the shed. He walked back to the car and pulled Sanya out and dragged her to the chair. He grabbed more rope and tied her to the chair.

Rosalia was looking at William and Sanya from behind the car.

Sanya felt William tie a cloth around her mouth, her teeth biting into the white fabric, and she felt it tighten around the back of her head. Sanya was soaked, water dripping down her face from the rain. She saw William go back into the shed and close the door. Rosalia crept around the car and stayed low, "Sanya?" she whispered. "I'm right here, okay, Sanya," she said in a low voice.

She saw Sanya nod her head slowly. Rosalia lay low as she waited for William to come out again.

William closed the door behind him as he entered the shed. He saw Sara, unconscious, tied up to the chair. She hadn't even tried escaping. William smirked, he grabbed a petrol can and took the cap off, he walked to Sara and poured some down her head. The petrol dripped down her face, and turned red as it passed by her cuts and wounds. She felt the petrol burn against her skin, and her eyes opened up She watched William pour more petrol on her; she couldn't speak. It was the *end.*

She was going to be gone.

William dropped the empty petrol can down and reached for the other one. He poured this one all around the small shed. Sara watched through her red eyes as the floor glistened with petrol. She heard the rain outside slow down; all she heard now was petrol pouring.

He grabbed another petrol can and stepped outside the shed. He poured petrol all around the outside.

Sanya sat still. She knew what was happening. William would throw her into the petrol-infused shed and set it on fire so she could die in it. He walked to her and pulled off the cloth from her mouth. Sanya let out a cough, "You're going to throw me in there, aren't you?" she said in a low whisper. William laughed, "No…well, not yet." Rosalia listened from behind the car. What *did he mean by not yet?*

William tossed the petrol cans away and grabbed his lighter from his pocket as he flicked it on, the red flames glowing in the dark evening. He stood in front of Sanya.

"If only *you* hadn't come into our house twenty years ago. If only my *stupid* mother had not decided to save *you* and bring *you* into *our* house. That's why my father got all pissed off at her. He thought *you* were a burden, so he hurt Mom. But then she died. Right in front of me. All because of *you.*"

Sanya tried to say something, but William interrupted, "Then of course *you had* to be there to see him kill her. And then *you* told me you would go to the police because *you* saw him kill Mom. But *you* never realised that since she died, he was all I had left? No. *You* wanted to be a good person and report it. You probably think I don't care about my mother dying. Well, news flash, I did. My father didn't mean to kill her; he was angry and got carried away. Because of *you,*" William shouted, pointing his shaking finger at Sanya.

Sanya was crying, tears flowing down her muddy face. William flickered the lighter on and off as he talked to Sanya, "Then I couldn't risk sending *you* back. I knew *you* would tell the police, so I had to think fast," he spoke, pointing his finger to his forehead, Williams eyes were red, the veins on his forehead looked like they were going to pop, turning a shade of green and blue. "I decided to lock *you* up in our basement. My father thought I should have just killed *you*, but I didn't, and then again, *you* were *never* grateful, were *you,* Sanya? I fed *you*. Brought *you* outside for *you* to clean up. *You* were living a good life for the past twenty years. But then *you* escaped. *Big, big mistake,*" he spoke with gritted teeth. "I had to make sure *you* wouldn't tell the police about all this. So, I kidnapped your sister. I locked her up in the same place *you* were rotting in. She was strong for a while, *you* know that? But then she got weaker and weaker."

Sanya felt her ears ring; she couldn't stop crying, "Where is she?" she shouted. William ignored her. "*You* should have just stayed in the basement, *you* should have stayed, Sanya. But of course, you decided to rebel and escape. *You* don't know how *scared* I was. Now that's going to cost you, and Sara."

Sanya watched as he flicked the lighter on and off; her eyes were getting blurry.

"*You* were supposed to be *gone*. The whole world was supposed to think *you* were *gone*. No one asked for *you* to come back, everyone forgot about *you,"* he shouted as he kicked Sanya's leg. She looked away, crying.

"Now even your sister is going to be *gone*, just like *you*"

"What, what do you mean?" Sanya asked, crying.

"*You* dug your own grave, Sanya. You should have never escaped."

"What are you doing?" she screamed

She watched him turn away as he walked to the shed. Rosalia stood up slowly, her eyes watery. She didn't know what she could do; she watched William open up the door, and she saw her.

She saw her.

Sara.

Sara Singh.

Her little sister.

After twenty years.

Sara.

Tied up to the chair, her hair matted, clothes bloody, eyes shut, and a cloth around her mouth, her head was swung over to the side, and she was breathing.

Rosalia sighed, tears streaming down her face, and she was breathing.

William opened the door completely, the sisters were now opposite to each other, tied up, Sanya stared at Sara, she looked just like she had imagined after all those years, her long eyelashes, olive skin, but Sara was covered in scars, cuts, bruises and blood, her eyes were shut, she was wet, but not because of water. Petrol. Sanya felt her heart beat faster. She screamed at William, "Don't- please, don't do anything to her, I'll go back, I'll never come out, just let her go, please."

"It's too late, Sanya, but since I'm a nice person, I'll let you say your goodbyes." William kicked Sara and pinched the side of her face. Her eyes struggling to open against the petrol on her face, she opened them and saw her.

She saw her.

Sanya.

Sanya Singh.

Her big sister.

After twenty years.

Sanya.

Chapter – 14

Not gone. Half gone.

Sara bit down on the cloth tied around her mouth. William untied it, “Any last words? Speak up.”

Sara didn't hear anything. She saw Sanya, tears filled her eyes as she let out a small smile, Sanya smiled back, “Sara,” she whispered as she stared into her little sister's deep, dark eyes, “Sanya,” cried Sara, her hands trembling against the rope they were tied to. “I’m sorry, Sara, you would have been fine if it wasn't for me, I should never have.”

“No, no, Sanya, look at me, it's not your fault, I’m just happy that I can see you… for the last time.”

Sanya smiled softly, her eyes crinkling. She hadn't smiled in a while. She stared at Sara's face, trying to take in everything before she was going to be burned to death by the man standing next to her.

“I love you, Sara,” she whispered. Sara replied in a soft voice, “I love you, big sis,” but William shushed them. “Enough small talk, now say your goodbyes, girls.”

William turned on the lighter and held his arm up to throw it on the cabin. He saw something from the corner of his eye, he turned and saw Rosalia standing up, her arms holding a metal pipe, “Oh my god, you again?” he rolled his eyes, putting the lighter down. "William, the police are coming; let them go, now."

"No"

"You'll go to jail, William, the police *will* find you, they *will* know you did this to them," Rosalia said, trying to keep her voice from shaking. Her fingers wrapped tightly around the rusted metal pipe she was holding.

William sighed, putting his lighter back into his pocket. Rosalia lowered the pipe she was holding.

It happened so fast.

I blinked my eyes, and I saw Rosalia fall to the floor, her arm bleeding out. Sanya was opposite me, a couple of feet away, and William was by my side.

I first saw him put his lighter away, then pull out a gun. I saw Rosalia's face turn white as he shot her arm. She fell backwards, screaming in pain. I shouted for her; her arm was bleeding out. William sighed like a maniac and put his gun away as he took out the lighter. He walked to the back of the cabin. I looked into Sanya's eyes, trying to register her face, so I could remember it, even after I burned. It was too early, I didn't want to die yet, and I just saw Sanya.

Rosalia was shouting in pain, Sanya was crying, and I heard police sirens in the distance. Then I heard William light the back of the shed on fire. He wanted it to be a slow burn. The back of the shed would burn first, then the flames would slowly come forward to me. Sanya would watch me burn. She was away from the shed.

William threw the burning lighter onto the back of the shed, which lit up instantly because of the petrol, he stepped back and ran to the front, he dragged Rosalia away and threw her into the car and he locked the car door, he saw her pound her fists against the car windows, as her left arm was bleeding against the inside of the car door. He heard police sirens. They would not come that fast. By the time they come, Sara would have burned in the fire, and after he made sure Sanya watched her burn, he would throw her in too. Then he would leave. No one would ever find him. They would find Rosalia in the car with a bullet in her arm. Sara and Sanya would be unrecognisable after they burned.

Then I'll run away, somewhere where no one ever finds me, and I'll change my name, everything. No one will ever know what happened. Rosalia will sound crazy if she says Sanya Singh is still alive after twenty years.

Rosalia tried to break out of the car, blood getting all over the windows, her fists banging against the glass. She held her arm in pain as she looked around the car for something to break out. She looked out and saw the flames coming closer and closer to Sara.

Sara was looking at Sanya, a small smile on her face.

Rosalia screamed, her eyes puffed up, she tried to kick the window down, but she could not; she heard her ankle crack, she screamed as she fell back onto the seat.

The flames got closer. And closer. They were a shade of dark orange. They looked beautiful in a strange way. Sanya saw the fire come closer and closer to Sara. The thick black smoke billowed and twisted through the air, swallowing what little was left of the evening light. Sara felt her chest close up from the smoke, her vision blurred, and she felt the heat come closer.

And closer.

And closer.

Ashes flew around, wood burning and crackling. Sanya's tears streamed down her face as she screamed. William watched from the side, Rosalia was shouting in the car.

Sara felt her chair tip over. She fell to the side, still tied tightly to the chair. She heard Sanya scream, and she saw red. All she saw was red; she heard the flames get closer.

And closer.

And closer.

Sara's eyes were blurry from tears and the smoke; she tried to open her eyes so she could see Sanya.

And closer.

And closer.

Sanya was trying to pull away from her chair, her wrists struggling against the thick rope. Rosalia cried. William was nowhere to be seen.

Sara felt the fire get closer.

And closer.

And closer.

Until it brushed against the back of her skin.

Her back burned, she heard flames burn deep in her ears and sirens. She saw red and blue lights in the distance, her eyes drifted to Sanya's, she mouthed, "I love you, Sanya", before her eyes closed.

The police ran out of the cars, frantically calling for more backup. Someone ran up to Sanya and untied her. She was screaming, "My sister, help her, please," with a broken voice.

They tried to pull Sanya away from the burning shed. She tried to run to me, but I heard her struggling, the police officers wouldn't even come close; they stood back, just watching in horror at the flames and me. I know they saw me burn; they couldn't help me. I heard Rosalia as they broke open the car door and let her out, she was crying, blood smeared all over her arm, "help her, go help her, why are you just watching, I said Go help-"

I heard more sirens. But it was too late. I was half burned, half gone. The firefighters arrived, trying to extinguish the scene. I felt someone pull my chair away from the fire. I heard Sanya shout, "Help her, please, help her."

I tried to open my eyes so I could see her once more, but they were sealed shut.

Then I didn't hear anymore.

I was gone.

Gone. Gone. Gone. Gone.

Completely gone.

Chapter – 15

"Please, help her," Sanya screamed, her voice breaking, again, as paramedics tried to calm her down, she broke free from them and ran to Sara, shaking her, "Wake up, wake up, Sara, please," she cried, her tears falling onto Sara, she felt someone grip onto her shoulders, it was a paramedic, "I'll take care of her, please move, ma'am," he said in a soft voice, Sanya didn't, listen, her eyes turning back to Sara, the next second she felt two strong arms pull her away from Sara, she saw paramedics try to resuscitate her.

Her back was burned, her skin was dark red and black, charred, flesh melting and peeling. Her eyes were shut, her mouth slightly open, her arms a shade of red. She still looked beautiful even with all the burn marks.

Sanya's cries grew louder, screaming her name again and again. She felt herself fall back in exhaustion, and she saw Rosalia run past her with blood dripping down her arm, her other hand clutching against the gunshot, leaving a trail next to Sanya.

Rosalia felt her eyes spin. She saw red ashes flying around the scene, police cars, crying, screaming, shouting, sirens. The scent of burnt wood and flesh hangs in the air.

Not half gone. Gone.

Gone.

Sara was gone.

Gone.

I saw Rosalia fall onto her knees and cry. They took Sara away. Someone held me up and took me into an ambulance. I watched the shed being burned down as firefighters extinguished it. Two paramedics brought a stretcher, they lifted Sara and put a white cloth over her, I felt my ears blur out all the sounds, the ambulance I was in started, and the doors shut slowly in front of me. It was all because of me. I did it. I should never have escaped from William.

William?

Where was he?

I turned to the paramedic next to me and held her by the shirt, "Stop, tell them to stop the ambulance, William escaped, I need to tell the police, I-"

"Ma'am, calm down, the police are handling it."

"Handling it? I was missing for twenty years, no one ever found me, do you think they will handle this?" I screamed.

The paramedic went silent. She lay me down, and I watched outside the windows as trees rushed past me. My head was throbbing. My eyes are blurry, my skin full of cuts and bruises.

Rosalia watched helplessly.

Sara was *gone*.

She saw her being taken away by the stretcher, blood soaking into the white cloth over her.

William. It was all because of him. She looked around and ran around the shed. The firefighters tried to stop her, but she had to find him; it was all because of him. She looked everywhere, she felt her arm hurt more and more with each second as it dripped bright red blood all over, she couldn't walk properly, her ankle was broken, she fell down, smoke slowly rose up, and ashes fell to the floor.

8:40 pm

I was in the police station, and they asked me questions. A lot. Millions of questions.

After they found out I was Sanya, the questions never stopped.

I would have liked some time alone.

But of course not. They wouldn't leave me alone this time like they did twenty years ago.

I saw Rosalia come into the station later. I ran up to her and hugged her. I think I might have crushed her bones. I didn't want to let go. She held me tightly, crying softly. We both had lost Sara. Forever. She was not going to come back, like how I did. She died. In front of my eyes. She would not just "reappear" like I did. I would do anything for her to come back, take my place, be alive instead of me. Anything.

The police went on a search for William. I told them everything. Rosalia was right next to me, holding my hand, never letting go.

Never letting go.

2 days later

They still didn't find William.

But they *will.*

I went back to the city with Rosalia. I stayed with her for a day. She said she would take me to Sara's apartment. We drove through the city in silence, the buildings blurred past us. I had to go back again, to Juniper Ridge, for more police questions. But I needed some time. Alone.

Rosalia dropped me at Sara's apartment, she took me upstairs, and told me to go in alone, she would give me space.

I stepped in, closing the door softly behind me.

It was like time had stopped. Soft evening light filled the house, orange light falling on the floor from the big glass windows.

I walked around, and I saw a picture hung up on the wall.

Sanya walked up to the picture, her eyes watery; it was an old picture of her family. Before everything happened.

My hand traced around little Sara in the picture, and I smiled softly.

I went into her bedroom, looking at all her pictures. She was just like I had imagined, an overachiever, but yet she made everything look so effortless. I sat down on her bed.

I wanted to see more pictures of her, to see what I had missed out on for twenty years. I looked around the room and found an old box filled with photos. Some of them were as old as before the accident. I flipped through them until an old paper, folded up, fell into my lap.

Chapter – 16

To Sanya.

November 15, 2005, Tuesday

I miss you.

I miss you so, so, so much. I really hope you come back. I wish you were still here with me. I turned eleven today, but it's no fun. I miss you and mumma and dad so much, it hurts everywhere. I've had this headache since the accident, and it won't go away. It's been more than a month since you disappeared. Mumma and dad died that day, I was crushed, I couldn't stop crying, the police asked me SO many questions, I don't really remember what they were, they kept on asking me if I saw which way you went, but all I remember is my eyes were closed and u let go of my hand, its ok, I know you have a reason for that, but it's just that I miss you, and I wish you had never let go of my hand. You're all I have left, Sanya. I wish you hadn't run off like that. But you did, and its ok, but I wish I held onto your hand tighter. I got hurt on my arms and back, but it's all fixed. The hospital kept me for about two weeks. I stayed with Aunty for a while, then with Grandma and Grandpa. Everyone felt so bad for me. Because they thought I was all alone. Forever. But I know you will come back. The police searched for you, but they still haven't found you. I really hope you come back. I have printed this letter out a lot of times and mailed it to all your favourite places, so if you're there, maybe you can come back. I really miss you, Sanya. You're the best older sister ever. Wherever you are, please come back. I printed out the address behind the paper. Please come back, wherever you are. I need you. Everything is so confusing. That day when that stupid lorry hit our car, I was so scared, I thought I was going to die. I don't want to die. The police said they finally found the guy who crashed into us; he was a drunk driver, and he's locked up in prison forever, but that doesn't change a thing. Mumma and Dad have gone. Forever. They can't come back. And you…I don't know where you are, Sanya. Everyone told me that I'd be okay, and this will all pass by. But I don't believe them, I don't think I'll ever be okay until I see you. They don't know what it's like to lose everyone you love all at once, all alone. I watched the news yesterday, and they were saying you died in the forest, because of the storm, but I know it's not true, you're so strong, a stupid storm won't kill you, not in a million years. Another news channel said you had run away to a whole different town to start a new life. It sounds stupid. I think I should stop watching the news. You're still out there, nothing will ever happen to you, and I know it, I know you're alright. I hope. I don't think I'll ever be able to live without you, Sanya. Even if you don't come back now, I know you will come back someday. You will. You will. You will. You will. You will. You will. You will. You will. And when you do, I'm going to hug you sooooo tight that you can't even breathe, I won't let go of you, at all, and I'll tell you how much I love you.

But for now, I'll wait forever, if I have to. I'll wait. I'll be patient. I love you.

Love,

Sara

Epilogue

Newspaper clipping from 2025

The Dispatch Daily

June 3, 2025

Mystery Unfolds After 20 Years: Sanya Singh Found Alive in Crimson Woods, Perpetrator Arrested

The long-lost case of Sanya Singh, who disappeared from a crime scene on September 21st, 2005, after running away from the car crash, has been found in Crimson Woods, near Hastings.

Sanya's ordeal began two decades ago when she vanished into Crimson Woods. She has claimed that William Burt, a police officer, held her captive in his own cabin in the woods. When Sanya was taken by his mother after she was found helpless in the woods, she witnessed a murder. The murder of Williams mother, Sanya claims she saw Williams' father kill his wife due to anger. William wanted to keep this under cover, to keep his father safe. After Sanya threatened to tell the police, he locked her up in the basement to silence her.

The story came to light when Sanya escaped two decades later; her escape caused William to take her sister, Sara Singh, a well-renowned surgeon. The terrifying climax occurred just days ago when William locked Sara up as well, to keep Sanya silent. Reports suggest that William tied Sara up in front of his shed as well as Sanya and lit the shed on fire. Sara Singh passed away due to burns and previous injuries. The paramedics arrived on scene and were unable to save her life. A police investigation was launched to find William Burt, and after a long week of searching, he was found hiding in a different town to the east of Hastings, with a changed name, working at a retail store. He has been arrested and is facing life in prison.

The funeral was quiet. Only Rosalia and I. We placed blue orchids in front of Sara's grave, and stood quietly, holding each other's hands, never letting go. I placed a little paper under the orchids.

A stupid storm never killed me. Thank you for being patient, thank you for waiting forever. I love you, Sara.

Sanya Singh